THE FEATS OF
SHERLOCK HOLMES

Six Lost Adventures of the World's

Greatest Detective

By Nick Cardillo

i

Paperback ISBN 978-1-78705-387-8
ePub ISBN 978-1-78705-388-5
PDF ISBN 978-1-78705-389-2

Published in the UK by MX Publishing
335 Princess Park Manor, Royal Drive,
London, N11 3GX
www.mxpublishing.co.uk

Cover design by Brian Belanger

Table of Contents

Forward

University libraries yield the most unexpected things.

Today, living in an age where we are so likely to use the Internet and the Internet alone to conduct research, the library – still the place for quiet contemplation amongst the stacks – has become overlooked. I suppose this makes the library's secrets all the more potent when it decides to divulge them. This manuscript is among those most unusual of discoveries.

I entered higher education with the intent of pursuing history. As a result, I found myself in need of primary documents more than most students on a small college campus. The library, therefore, became my home away from home. And, certainly, there could be worse places to spend your time. Unlike a small dormitory, the library was spacious. It was quiet (in a library some boy from down the hall is not playing music at two o'clock in the morning). And, above all, it was *interesting*.

Being a history major, I cultivated a group of friends with the same interest. Some of them even found on-campus jobs working in the library's archives which, despite my best intentions, I never found myself in. That was until I received a text message which changed my life forever.

One spring morning, I was walking out of class, encountering the brisk, cool air of central Pennsylvania once again, and checking my phone, I discovered that I had received a message while I had had my phone on silent. It was from a close friend of mine – one who worked in the library's archives – and she had posed to me a single question: *What was the name of Sherlock Holmes's friend?*

Of course, I knew the answer better than I knew the back of my own hand. I had made it abundantly clear from day one to just about anyone that I encountered that I was a Sherlock Holmes fanatic and had been since the days of my childhood. I had fallen under the detective's spell at once when I read the *Great Illustrated Classics* edition of *The Adventures of Sherlock Holmes*. From the day that I first started that book I wanted to know what the secret of the Red-Headed League was; I yearned to know what those mysterious, haunting last words "the speckled band" could possibly mean; and I trembled with the same anxiety that Violet Hunter did when she discovered a length of auburn hair in her drawer in "The Copper Beeches." In short order, a family friend introduced me to the (rightfully) much-beloved Granada television series starring Jeremy Brett as Holmes, and from there I took the deep dive into the Canon itself. I became known throughout much of my life as a walking, talking encyclopedia of Sherlockian knowledge, and therefore and I felt a bit of pride that morning when I received that message in hopes that I could help answer someone's Holmes-related quandary.

I texted back at once: *Dr. John H. Watson.*

I sent another message immediately afterward – mainly because I simply could not help myself: *The H stands for Hamish. Or, so we think.*

I received a reply faster than I would have anticipated: *You've got to come to the archives.*

Then another: *NOW.*

I had some free time before my next class and, being close enough to the library, I figured that there was little that I could lose. I made for the library right away and, descending into the basement, met my friend outside of the archive room. At first, I must admit, I was a little disappointed to find that the room was not the kind of dusty, claustrophobic room that archives are made out to be on TV; the sort where the answer to some arcane problem is discovered stuffed in the bottom of some cardboard box perched high on a wrought-iron shelf. Instead, I was greeted with an average-sized room with a few computers, a table and chairs, a few boxes, and a large file sitting on the conspicuously empty tabletop.

In dark lettering embossed on the top of the old, weathered stack of pages, I divined a few words which had not been lost to the sands of time:

John H. Watson M.D. (retd)
Formerly of Fifth Northumberland Fusiliers

"Oh my god," I said, my voice catching in my throat.

I had barely uttered another syllable before my friend was pushing a pair of latex gloves into my hands.

"We've examined it pretty closely," she said, "and it appears to be genuine. I figured that you should be one of the first people to see this."

I didn't know how else to react other than to throw myself into her arms and giving her a very warm hug – my chosen reaction eliciting a great laugh.

Over the course of the next few weeks, I made many trips to that archive room. First, I was there simply to read over the manuscript. I took it at first to be a series of first-drafts for many of the published Sherlock Holmes adventures, but I discovered very quickly that this was something very different. These stories had never seen the light of day. As soon as I realized what I had in front of me, I ran out to my local office supplies store and invested in more legal pads than I knew what to do with.

And that is how that manuscript has made its way into your hands.

I should take a moment to apologize in advance. The pages were quite old and, though in fairly decent shape for their age, they were by no means perfect. The writing was hard to decipher in places and in others, the sheets of foolscap were so worn that lines or paragraphs were nearly incomprehensible. There has, therefore, been some dramatic license taken in the putting-back-together of these six stories as I tried to put myself in Watson's shoes and determine how he might have told this story.

When I came to the end of this long road, I was left with one question above all the others: how did these stories end up in the basement archive of a small university in Pennsylvania. Try as I might to apply Holmes's logic and deductive reasoning to that question, I could not come to a conclusion which I deemed satisfactory nor one which I thought fit all of the facts. Perhaps, after a bit more digging, I can conclusively answer that problem which perturbs me still.

But, isn't life just a little richer with those unexplained happenings, I ask myself. Maybe this is a case where not having an answer just makes the whole thing just a little more intriguing.

And, if nothing else, this manuscript proves once and for all that you never know what you're liable to find inside your library.

Nick Cardillo

2018

Introduction by John H. Watson M.D.

During my long and intimate friendship with Mr. Sherlock Holmes, there were a number of occasions when we handled cases of a sensitive or potentially scandalous nature. These problems I knew could never be presented to the public, even if I did change names and dates to protect those involved as I so often did. Come the conclusion of one of these exploits, and Holmes and I would find ourselves ensconced in the comforts of 221b Baker Street once more; he in his chair before the fire wreathed in a thick fog of pipe smoke, while I sat at my desk ready to put pen to paper and transcribe the case while its particulars were still fresh in my mind.

"No, Watson," Holmes would tell me without even having to turn in my direction, "perhaps it is best that this story not see publication."

"But, Holmes," I would insist, "the world has a right to know of your amazing intellect. Surely, Scotland Yard would have yet again been lost without you."

"Be that as it may," my friend would counter, "I fear that for all of your changes to history, the public would see right through it. They are more perceptive than you often give them credit for, my dear fellow. And I rather think that we have enough to contend with. This agency need not face charges of libel on top of the thieves, murderers, and swindlers we deal with on a day-to-day basis."

He was, of course, right and I would put aside my pen in surrender.

"You need not give up though," Holmes would continue. "Make a record for posterity if you so desire. But, like so many of your other manuscripts, you must consign it to some obscure corner of the Cox and Company Bank vault. Perhaps, one day Watson, you can make a full account of it, but not today."

And that is precisely what I have done. It was not without some resistance that I take these stories and prevent them from ever seeing the light of day. They – like so much of my other work – showcase Holmes's incredible gifts. Yet he remains adamant, and as my communication with him has lessened in the days since he has found solace amongst his bees on the Sussex Downs, I feel that it is unlikely that I should hear otherwise from him.

Perhaps, though, as Holmes said, they can one day be revealed to the world, but until then they shall remain my own private record of the Feats of Mr. Sherlock Holmes.

John H. Watson, M.D.
1905

The Plain Gold Wedding Ring

The August of '82 was dry, a relief following a spell of rain during the earlier summer months which had shut both Sherlock Holmes and I indoors. The pleasant weather had brought about in me great joy, and I set about opening the windows to our Baker Street rooms and basking in the warm air which blew in. Holmes, on the other hand, seemed to take little solace in it. Surely, if I had pressed him on the subject he would have told me that a change in weather would have had little bearing on him and that he could apply his methods of observation and deduction in any set of circumstances.

I should not have found such a response to be uncharacteristic of my friend in that period. Though Holmes had had a fruitful summer, occupied with a number of cases, nothing out of the ordinary had caught his attention. He would often spend his mornings perusing the agony columns of *The Times* in hopes of catching a whiff of some queer business to which he could apply his abilities. However, he seemed to deem nothing beyond the commonplace. It is, for that reason, that had I not intervened one morning, I daresay the case which I am about to draw up might never have come to my friend's attention.

It was at the conclusion of breakfast one sunny morning and Holmes and I were both seated in silence, the papers draped across our knees. I heard Holmes groan under his breath and toss the paper aside.

Looking up from the column of text, I perceived my friend leaning back in his chair, reaching his long, nervous fingers for his cigarette case at his side.

"You know, Watson," Holmes said as he lit a cigarette, "sometimes I envy you."

"Oh? Why is that?"

"You and the rest of this city," Holmes replied setting the burnt out match into an ashtray already overflowing with the remains of its brethren and long-since smoked cigarettes, "live such simple lives. Granted, your lives are tedious in their simplicity, but you are not like me. You're content to peruse the paper, take in the weather, and go on your merry way. How I sometimes wish I could relinquish myself of my powers and live out the life of a *simpleton*."

"That is unworthy of you, Holmes," I said, taken aback by his words. Holmes waved his hand dismissively.

"You know I mean nothing by it. You are a catalyst, Watson. You incite in me some of my finer moments of mental acuity. A true conductor of light. But, you must confess that you are content this morning?"

"I am," I replied. "As you should be too. You have successfully completed three cases in as many weeks. I'd like to see Lestrade, Gregson, or Jones at the Yard do as much."

Holmes snorted. "You are also endowed with the remarkable ability to put things into perspective, my fine fellow. Bravo!"

I bowed slightly in my chair.

"Nevertheless," Holmes continued, "I yearn for something *grander* than what I have been involved with of late. I crave a mental exercise of a considerably more challenging variety."

Holmes had said just as much when the bell rang below. A moment later, Mrs. Hudson, our landlady, knocked politely and informed us that a woman had called upon us. Holmes pressed her to join us and Mrs. Hudson returned with an elderly woman in tow. I took her to be in her late sixties or very early seventies and, despite the warm temperatures outside, she was bundled up as she shuffled into our rooms. Holmes and I stood as we greeted the elderly caller.

"Thank you very much for seeing me, Mr. Holmes," she said.

"I shall assist you in any way that I can, madam," Holmes replied as he gestured for our visitor to take a seat on the settee. Holmes returned to his own chair. "Your name, madam?"

"My name is Hilda Devereux," the old woman replied. "And I have come about my granddaughter, Mary."

"Pray, tell me everything, Mrs. Devereux," Holmes said, "and omit nothing, no matter how inconsequential you may perceive it."

Settling back in his chair, Holmes pressed his fingertips together in his habitual, contemplative manner. I reached for my notebook and pen.

"I do not wish you to believe that the matter which brings me to you is one of great consequence," Mrs. Devereux began. I cast Holmes a sideways glance and could see an air of disappointment descend over him. Though, I am sure, he thought that this old woman was not bringing to his door a case of national security, I doubt that I would be far off the mark in suggesting that Holmes had the highest of hopes for any potential case. "You may chalk my visit up to the over-protectiveness of an old woman," Mrs. Devereux continued. "You see, I am like a mother to my granddaughter, Mary.

"My daughter died in childbirth some nineteen years ago. I felt a moral obligation following the death of my daughter's husband to take in Mary and raise her as my own. My husband, Percival, and I have done everything that we can to ensure that Mary gets as far in life as she can. We are not wealthy people, Mr. Holmes, but we made sure that Mary received a quality education and, in two years' time, we very much suspect that she could make a first-class governess. However, what brings me to your door today is Mary's impending marriage and the man to whom she is betrothed."

"You have some doubts about him?" I inquired.

"Not in the least, doctor," Mrs. Devereux replied. "The young man – two years her senior and named Kenneth Patterson – is a fine specimen. He is of a completely upstanding character and has few, if any vices. Both Percival and I have given the marriage our total blessing and we could not be happier for Mary."

"Then, what is it that concerns you about this young man?"

Mrs. Devereux reached into the small bag which she held in her hands and withdrew a plain, gold wedding band. Leaning forward, she pressed it into Holmes's hand. "This is the ring which Kenneth gave to Mary for their engagement. It is a simple, plain gold wedding ring as you can very well see. Kenneth is not of a wealthy disposition either, so the ring's commonplace nature is not of any concern to me. But, I am no expert, Mr. Holmes; can you tell if it is real?"

Holmes raised both of his eyebrows. "You wish me to *authenticate* this ring?"

Hilda Devereux nodded anxiously. "I do apologize if the matter is beneath you, Mr. Holmes. But, as I said, I am no expert in jewelry and I am very protective of Mary. I have taken care of her since the day she was born. She is like another daughter to me."

It was now Holmes's turn to shoot me the sidelong glance. This development, I could read in his face, was an obvious disappointment. After what seemed like an age, Holmes stood from his chair.

"I have exactly what it takes to determine this ring's authenticity here," Holmes said as he took a seat at his chemical workbench.

Taking up a Petri dish, Holmes placed the ring into the small glass saucer. He then reached for an unmarked bottle and slowly inserted a dropper into the bottle. He then held the pipette over the ring and dropped a few drops of the liquid onto the ring. Waiting a moment, Holmes sat back in the chair and folded his arms in a satisfied manner.

"That bottle," he said, "contained nitric acid. When it comes into contact with a metal other than genuine gold, it will turn the metal green. Should I have observed a cloudy reaction, I would have been able to deduce that your ring is actually made of gold-plated sterling silver. That, in itself, does hold some value, but cannot hold a candle to the value of genuine gold. However, as neither of those two reactions occurred, I can confidently tell you, Mrs. Devereux, that that ring is quite genuine."

Using a rag, Holmes picked up the ring and dipped it into a small cup of water. Drying it, he returned the ring to Mrs. Devereux and settled into his chair once more. The expression of pure joy which the old woman wore was not difficult to read.

"You are sure that it is real, Mr. Holmes?"

"Beyond a shadow of a doubt," Holmes replied. "There are a number of other simple methods which I could have utilized; however the application of nitric acid is, perhaps, the most foolproof method of which I know. I hope that I have taken some weight from your shoulders."

"You cannot possibly know, Mr. Holmes."

Holmes smiled. "Your maternal instincts are most understandable, Mrs. Devereux. Before you go, however, I should very much like to ask you one or two questions."

The old woman sat back in her seat.

"Do you know the name of the jewelry shop at which the young Mr. Patterson purchased this ring?"

"The shop was called Forbes and Sons," Mrs. Devereux replied. Holmes told me to make a note of the name.

"While I am sure that your concern for the well-being of your granddaughter was what prompted you to visit me this morning, was there some other reason that you suspected that this ring was not genuine gold?"

"I knew that Kenneth was by no means a wealthy man," the woman replied. "When I saw the ring that he was able to get for Mary, I became concerned that it was not the genuine article. You hear horror stories you know, Mr. Holmes, of young men who are liable to pick up cheap rings in pawnshops. If they are willing to do such a thing to a testament of their love, what will they be like as actual husbands? And…well, there was something else."

"Please, continue, Mrs. Deveraux," Holmes insisted. "I told you that I should like to hear all of the details concerning this business, no matter how trivial you may consider them."

"Well," Mrs. Devereux said drawing in a deep breath, "when I learned that Kenneth had purchased the ring from Forbes and Sons I did become worried. You see, a dear friend of mine, Mrs. Agatha Cushing, purchased some jewels from the very same shop only a fortnight ago. I found them to be quite marvelous items, so much so that I almost considered paying a visit to the shop myself. I am not one for jewelry, but I simply could not resist. Those hopes were dashed only a week later when I learned from Agatha that her jewels were imitation."

"Mrs. Cushing had purchased fake jewels from the very same shop that Kenneth Patterson bought that ring from?" I asked.

"Precisely, doctor," Mrs. Devereux responded. "Naturally, that put me on edge. My fears were compounded when Kenneth purchased the ring around the very same time that Agatha discovered her jewels were fake. I cannot begin to imagine what transpired to have caused such a mishap to befall Agatha, but I could not help but cast some suspicion on the shop itself. And, if that were the case, I could not very well return to them to authenticate the ring. What if they were complicit in selling Agatha some imitation jewelry? Surely they would try to do the same to me?"

"Your skepticism is very natural, Mrs. Devereux," I said. "At any rate, however, I think that you need not concern yourself with this ring any longer. Should Mr. Holmes and I wish to contact you again, where might we be able to find you?"

Mrs. Hilda Devereux supplied us with her address and made her way out of the room beaming all the while. Holmes was curiously silent as our caller turned and left. Once I had returned to the sitting room having shown her out to a cab, he went about lighting another cigarette. Losing him in a haze of cigarette smoke, I heard him murmur as I returned to my seat:

"Why did you do that?"

"Do what?" I asked.

"Ask for her address? The case is completed, Watson. It was a simple matter occupying only five minutes of my time. I simply asked a few questions for my own edification."

"But does it not strike you as odd," I began, "that the very same shop which sold Kenneth Patterson a genuine ring would sell another woman fake jewels only one week earlier? I cannot understand it."

"I would suspect that there is a great deal which you do not understand, Watson," Holmes retorted. I could tell that he was slowly beginning to regard the morning's activity as a waste of his time. "There are a number of explanations; the simplest is that Mrs. Agatha Cushing's jewels *weren't* imitation at all. Perhaps, wearing them to some kind of social gathering, a boor who couldn't tell the difference between The Regent and The Hope Diamond, made the declaration that Mrs. Cushing's jewels were fakes. With nothing to refute the statement, Mrs. Cushing went along with the story and fell into hysterics."

"You know as well as I that that argument rests on nothing but conjecture," I rebuked. "Holmes," I added trying to calm my simmering temper, "you are endlessly telling me how you crave mental stimulation. You have been presented with a case! And, you cannot deny that the particulars of this venture are not common. At least make a visit to Forbes and Sons Jewelry Shop. You have nothing to lose but time."

Holmes steepled his fingers and drew in a deep breath. After some length of time, he said:

"You really do have the most remarkable persuasive capabilities. And, though I have already been forced to admit it once this morning, your power of perspective is unrivaled."

Holmes rose from his seat, crushing the cigarette into the ashtray.

"Then you shall investigate?"

"I shall," Holmes replied. "And, I should very much hope that you join me. I am unfamiliar with Forbes and Sons. Curious, really. But we shall rectify that in time. Come, let us be off. If nothing else, we can partake in some luncheon."

In short order, Holmes and I were wading through the city streets of London, weaving in and out of the crowds who had emerged from their haunts to take in the sun and warm air. Dressed in a light suit with straw boater hat, jauntily swinging his stick, Holmes looked very much the part of a young member of the aristocracy. I had not gone as far in attiring myself for the weather, but I had divested myself of my greatcoat which, in the winter months, became very much like an outer layer of skin.

Our walk was a pleasant one. We spoke together of the fine weather and the shops we passed; Holmes's remarkable knowledge of London was only beginning to be impressed upon me. Before we had even rounded a street corner, he had rattled off the shops which lined the boulevard, leaving me in a state of some stupefaction. These were still early days for Holmes and I, and I was ever becoming more aware of the complex constituent parts which went to making up that remarkable man.

We soon found ourselves stepping off of the main thoroughfare and ducking into a picturesque side street. It was narrow, lined on both sides by shops, each adorned with lamps which, I am sure in the night, would cast a lovely golden halo around the stores' front entrances. Holmes had jotted the address to the jewelers on his shirt cuff before we had left Baker Street and, as we approached, he pointed with his stick at the handsome sign which hung over the doorway. Though the shop was one of some standard, I fear that it would be too much to call the un-prepossessing abode as one of out-and-out fashion. It was a simple building done over in stone with two windows in which stood a few showcases drawing attention to some of the shop's most handsome wares.

"My choice of wardrobe was not unintentional this afternoon, Watson," Holmes said. "I saw your eyebrows arch when I emerged from my room looking not unlike a pretentious fop. That is precisely the image I wished to present to the owners of this place. I hazard that my name does carry some weight in the criminal classes and, should there be anything untoward conducted here, I fear that a call from Sherlock Holmes might put them on edge. Disguise, my friend, is oftentimes about hiding in plain sight."

So saying, Holmes approached the door to the building and opened it, stepping inside. I followed dutifully at his heels. The shop was small, but well-appointed; jewels were displayed in a number of ornate glass cabinets. What was not housed in glass stood behind the main counter which was situated near the back of the shop behind which presided a young, fair-haired, fresh-faced man. He greeted us warmly as I closed the door behind me.

"Can I be of assistance to you gentlemen?" he asked.

"No, no," Holmes replied haughtily. "We're just here to have a quick look about. I have heard that you have some fine pieces for a most reasonable price."

"You have heard quite right," the young man replied.

Holmes continued to look around the shop imitating a patron going about scrutinizing the jewels with care. I followed suit, though I daresay my charade was not as convincing as Holmes's. At length, Holmes called me to his side as he pointed to a simple gold band which stood within a glass case.

"Does that item draw your attention, Watson?" he asked.

Indeed it did. The ring was nearly identical to the one which Mrs. Hilda Devereux had shown us earlier that morning.

"Young man," Holmes called, "could we see this ring here, please?"

The young man approached us, opened the glass case and handed us the ring. Holmes turned it over in his fingers and held it before his eye, poring over it with the most involved concentration.

"We shall put your claims to the test," Holmes said. "You say that your prices are reasonable. How much for this ring?"

"One pound," the young man replied.

Holmes grinned. "Not an unreasonable price in the least," he said. Withdrawing a coin from his pocket, he handed it to the young man. In response, the young man removed a ledger from behind the counter and had Holmes sign. Peering over his shoulder, I noted that he scribbled the name 'John Watson' as well as an address to a club in Whitehall. Once the ring was in Holmes's possession, he asked the young man, "You are the proprietor of the shop?"

"No," the young man replied. "That would be my father."

"Then you are one of the sons in Forbes and Sons," I interjected.

"Exactly, sir," the young man replied. By way of an introduction, he added, "Benjamin Forbes, at your service."

"Rest assured Mr. Forbes," Holmes said, "I shall be frequenting this shop again in the future. You sell lovely items and, unlike some jewelry shops, I do not get the distinct impression that you're robbing me blind." Holmes laughed at his own jest. "Well, allow us to be off. Have a pleasant afternoon, Mr. Forbes."

Holmes turned and started out of the shop. Once we were outside, the detective extracted the ring from his inner pocket again and examined it. "I promised you a meal, Watson," he said. "After lunch, however, I have one or two tests which I wish to conduct on this ring as well. But, come. I'd wager we are early enough to take advantage of a lull at Marcini's."

We spoke little of the case during lunch and returned to Baker Street shortly after two o'clock in the afternoon. Holmes set about taking a seat at his chemical workbench as I stood by, interested to see what his tests concluded. First, he selected a graduated cylinder from amongst a rack of test tubes and beakers and, filling it with water, dropped the ring into the cylinder. I watched my friend analyzed the meniscus closely before he poured the water away and dried the ring on a rag. He then reached for a Petri dish and bottle of nitric acid just as he done that morning. He repeated the process of slowly drawing a few drops of the acid into a pipette and dropping them onto the ring. When he had finished, I heard him murmur something inaudibly beneath his breath. Washing the ring off, Holmes turned about on his stool and tossed the ring into my hands. I rushed to catch it.

"You need not concern yourself with that," Holmes said. "It's a fake."

"What?" I exclaimed.

"I conducted two tests to make certain that I was correct," Holmes said. "You know as well as I do that gold is one of the densest elements and, therefore, when dropped into a graduated cylinder, will displace water. Little visible displacement was observed when I did just that. And, when I performed the same nitric acid test that I ran on Mrs. Devereux's ring, I found that it turned slightly green in color. That ring is an imitation through and through."

"But…I don't understand," I stammered as Holmes stood and crossed to his own chair. He took a seat, languidly crossing one leg over the other. "Why should a shop sell both fake jewels alongside the genuine article without advertising the fact?"

"Ah, that is the question of the hour, Watson," Holmes replied. "It may very well be a quirk of the shopkeepers, but I think not." From his waistcoat, Holmes withdrew his watch. "It is very nearly three," he said. "Let us enjoy the solitude for a few hours and then, tonight, let us decamp to Mrs. Devereux's. I think it would do us both some good to meet the young Kenneth Patterson and Mary Devereux."

We did just as Holmes suggested and we sat in the relative quiet of the sitting room; I content to lose myself in a novel which had sat unopened on my shelf for some time, while Holmes paged through the papers and smoked cigarette after cigarette. Mrs. Hudson furnished us with dinner and, shortly after the dishes were cleared away, Holmes and I took up our hats and sticks once more and hailed a hansom cab. Our journey took us to a quaint, but by no means prosperous corner of the city. We flitted from our cab and strode towards the neat little home of the Devereux's which was situated in a row of similar-looking dwellings. Holmes rang the bell and it was answered a moment later by a white-haired man who peered at us from behind a delicate pair of pince-nez.

Holmes introduced ourselves and the man's face lightened immediately and he shook us both by the hand. "My wife told me that she was going to seek out your services, Mr. Holmes," the man said. "My name is Percival Devereux. Please, please, come in!"

Mr. Devereux ushered us into the house. He called out to his wife as we entered a small parlor furnished with a simple settee and chair which sat before an unlit fireplace. Mrs. Devereux looked up, surprised as we entered the room.

"Mr. Holmes, Dr. Watson. Whatever do I owe this pleasure?"

"Dr. Watson and I are following up on a few loose strands in your case, Mrs. Devereux," Holmes replied. "Just this afternoon we visited Forbes and Sons' shop for ourselves."

"And did you learn anything of importance?"

I was about to tell the old woman and her husband of our findings when Holmes interjected:

"Nothing of consequence, I'm afraid," Holmes said. "The shop seemed to me to be a legitimate one operated by the most amiable young man."

Mr. Devereux smiled. "I for one am certainly glad to hear it," he said. "I like that young Patterson chap. He's just the man for Mary. I knew he wouldn't buy a ring from a place if it weren't on the *up-and-up* as it were."

"Do you expect Mr. Patterson to be coming here anytime soon?" Holmes asked.

Mrs. Devereux nodded. "He and Mary are out now. I should expect them to be back soon. Do you wish to meet him?"

"I should like nothing more," Holmes answered. "Dr. Watson and I have heard so much about him; it's almost as if we know the man already."

The Devereuxs offered to fetch us some nourishment and, though Holmes and I protested, they would not accept no for an answer. Leaving us to ourselves for a moment, I turned to Holmes and asked him why he wished to keep the news about the imitation ring to himself.

"There's no need to concern Mrs. Devereux in that way," he replied. "If my intuition is accurate – as it usually is – there is something larger at stake here than first meets the eye. I am certain that this trifling little matter goes far beyond a simple, gold wedding band and I am determined to find out just what is happening here – even if that means having to while away the evening in the company of the Devereuxs."

Percival Devereux returned to the sitting room carrying two glasses which he pressed into our hands. "Excuse the cup, doctor," he said. I noticed that he had poured my libation not into the typical tumbler, but rather a cup and saucer. "Something extraordinary happened this afternoon and, well…the glass which matches the one which Mr. Holmes is now holding was broken."

"*Something extraordinary?*" Holmes asked. "Do explain, Mr. Devereux."

Percival Devereux eased back in his chair and raised his glass to his lips. "Well, it has been hot out these past few days," he began, "so I suppose I really ought not to be too surprised by what happened. All-the-same, I was in here – I do confess enjoying an early-afternoon snifter of brandy – when I heard Hilda come along outside. She had inserted the key into the lock of the front door when her attention was arrested by a young man. From what she told me, the young chap said he was feeling faint being out in the sun and was practically begging for a glass of water. My wife, the charitable woman that she is, could not very well turn him down for such a simple request. And that's when he fell into her arms."

Mr. Devereux took another sip from his drink. "My wife is a stalwart woman, gentleman, but I could hear her shrieking from the other side of the door and knew something was amiss. So, I rushed to open the door and found her on the stoop cradling the young man. It took us some effort, but we managed to pull him in here and prop him up in a chair. I poured him a glass of brandy to bring him 'round and, though rather groggy, he was back in the land of the living. He still insisted on that glass of water however. My wife went to fetch it and, while she was out of the room, the boy complained about a severe headache and tumbled out of the chair. He struck the table on his way down, upsetting the glass. The glass fell to the ground and shattered. Naturally, my concerns weren't for that glass. Hilda and I propped the young man up again and settled back in the chair and it was at that point that I went to fetch a doctor."

"Was anything wrong with the young man?" I asked.

"According to Dr. Corey who has an office just down the road, nothing seemed to be at all wrong with the young man. But, I suppose you would know as well as any other man, Dr. Watson, that the heat can do strange things with a man's head."

"Dizzy spells are not at all uncommon in extreme heat," I replied. "Nevertheless, it is quite shocking that that happened to you and your wife. And with a complete stranger too."

Mrs. Devereux bustled into the room. "Ah, I heard my husband telling you about the theatrics which transpired in this very room today."

"A most extraordinary turn of events," Holmes said. "Tell me, what did this man look like?"

"Oh, he was a young man," Mrs. Devereux answered. "He was perhaps only a year or two older than Kenneth. He was dressed in a heavy coat and hat. I, myself, was somewhat heavily bundled up this morning, but I'm an old woman. A fresh-faced lad that like oughtn't to have been wearing so heavy a garment in such warm weather."

"I am sure that that did not help him at all," I replied.

It seemed as though we were to continue going around and around in circles discussing the matter further, when we heard the door open and two voices in the foyer. A young couple swept into the room a moment later. The lady was a petite, brown-haired young woman. There was a decided resemblance between her and old Mrs. Devereux. I knew at once that this was Mary Devereux, but I could not help but marvel at how handsome she was. The man at her arm was taller and broad-shouldered. Well-dressed in an inexpensive suit, I took him to be Kenneth Patterson. He too was quite a handsome figure in his own right.

Mrs. Devereux introduced the young couple to Holmes and me in turn. Mary informed her grandmother that she and Patterson had taken in a show at a music hall before a walk through the park. Going off into the next room as though they were about to gossip like a couple of schoolgirls, Kenneth Patterson took a seat next to myself on the settee as Holmes rose and lighted a cigarette.

"I must admit that I have heard your name before," Patterson said to Holmes. "Your reputation precedes you."

"You are far too kind," Holmes said without much humility. "I too must admit something myself: the reason for visiting the Devereuxs this evening was to meet you."

"I don't know whether to be flattered or not," Patterson said. "Have I done anything wrong?"

"Not in the slightest," Holmes replied. "However, if you could tell me all you know about Forbes and Sons Jewelers, it would be much appreciated."

"I wish that I could tell you more than I can, Mr. Holmes," Patterson replied. "You see, I only went there after hearing from a few of the chaps that I work with that they had nice jewelry for an inexpensive price. I wanted to get an engagement ring for Mary, but I am hardly the wealthiest of men. Working as the clerk in a shipping office is not the most lucrative of positions."

"Had you ever visited the place before?"

"Never. If you need a list of the boys who told me to go –"

"You need not trouble yourself, Mr. Patterson," Holmes replied. "I appreciate you taking the time to answer a few questions." Holmes glanced at his watch. "Dr. Watson and I have occupied too much of your time as it stands, Mr. Devereux. We shall show ourselves out. Thank you again."

Holmes drew out of the room quickly leaving me to thank the Devereuxs once more and apologize for my friend's lack of common courtesy. I found him in the street outside tapping his stick impatiently upon the ground.

"Don't tell me that this evening was wasted, Holmes," I said as though I were reprimanding a wayward child.

"On the contrary," Holmes replied. "I am of the opinion that much was gained from this evening's sojourn. Tomorrow, however, I believe shall be a day spent at Baker Street. I will need to send a few telegrams on the way home. And, we ought to stop at the tobacconist. I cannot very well spend my day indoors without a pipe or two."

I rose early the following morning. I breakfasted alone. I knew that Holmes anticipated a long day before him and I knew that it would be best not to wake him. After I had finished, I decided to take advantage of yet another beautiful summer day. I started out on a short walk and, having traversed my familiar path, I returned to our rooms. As I opened the door to the sitting room, I was surprised to see that Holmes had a guest. He was seated in my customary seat before the fireplace. He was a young man, perhaps only a year or two older than Holmes and looked not unlike my friend. He was nearly as tall, lean, and gaunt as the detective, but atop his hawk-like head was a mop of blonde hair which had already begun to prematurely grey. Upon my entrance, Holmes's face brightened.

"Ah, Watson, how good of you to join us. Allow me to introduce you to someone who owed me a favor: Algernon North."

I balked at the peculiar name. I could see the ghost of a smile creep across our guest's however. "Sherlock," our visitor said, languidly crossing his leg over the other, "is being just as unsociable as ever. While he perceives me simply as *someone who owed him a favor*, you and I, doctor, might go so far as to call me a *friend*."

"I am afraid," I said taking a seat on the settee, "that your name is unfamiliar to me, Mr. North."

"I have not spoken to you of Algernon North for one particular reason, Watson," Holmes said. "North is one of my many contacts in the criminal classes of London. He is by trade a thief."

I fear that I must have blanched for our caller laughed. "You need not fear, Dr. Watson. Picking the lock of 221b Baker Street and making off with your valuables is hardly at the top of my list of priorities."

I chuckled nervously. Though it would become not uncommon for members of London's criminal fraternity to take a seat in our Baker Street rooms, this was one of the first times that I could recall it occurring. I admit that I felt awkward and on edge, even though our visitor seemed to be the perfect gentleman.

"Now then," North said at length, "perhaps, Sherlock, you could get around to telling me exactly *why* you have called me here. You've been quite cryptic...as usual."

From the table at his side, Holmes plucked up the golden ring which we had procured yesterday afternoon and handed it across to North. Algernon North squeezed a monocle into his eye and scrutinized the ring minutely before handing it back to Holmes.

"It's a fake," he said. "I do hope you are not disappointed."

"I knew that it was a fake," Holmes rebuked. "I hoped that you might recognize it."

"It's hardly out-of-the-ordinary," North responded, surprised by my friend's words. "Now, if it had been a real ring, I fancy that it might have been worth something. It's imitation fourteen carat gold. Worth a pretty penny I should imagine."

"Although you do not recognize the ring offhand," Holmes said, "perhaps you can still be of service. What can you tell me of any jewel robberies which have been kept from the public? I'm interested only in those which may have occurred within the past month."

A grin crossed Algernon North's face. "Ah," he said, "now I see why it pays to have a friend in the criminal underworld of London." North paused for a moment and considered. "There has only been one of any great interest. A skillful job too, I will admit. Though, you need not fear, Doctor, I was not involved.

"No, the one to which I refer would be the purloining of an entire jewelry box from the room of Mrs. Arabella Hargreaves, wife of a diplomat who was staying at The Langham Hotel. An investigation was launched...oh, perhaps...three weeks ago, but nothing has turned up yet. I have been on the look-out for the jewels myself. I have heard that they are quite extraordinary."

"Why have the police not released the details of the case?" I asked.

"It was at the insistence of Mr. Hargreaves and his wife," North replied. "As I understand it, the Hargreaves' are wealthy diplomats from somewhere in the southern United States. And, you know how Americans are – they take to scandal even more than we do. I believe that the Hargreaves' were concerned with the possible scandal which could come about if word got out that Mrs. Hargreaves' jewels were snatched right from under her nose."

"No leads have been made in the case?" Holmes asked coldly.

"I hardly know every detail of Scotland Yard's case, Sherlock," North rebuked. "That is far more your department than mine."

"Perhaps, then, you at least know *who* is leading this investigation?"

"Ah, that I do know. As I understand it, Mr. Tobias Gregson is in charge of the investigation." Holmes chortled. "Oh, you know the fellow, do you?" asked North.

"Gregson and I have crossed paths on a few occasions," Holmes answered.

Holmes rose from his chair to bid our visitor farewell. Algernon North rose and shook Holmes warmly by the hand leaving my friend looking a little bewildered by the action. North did the same to me and swept out of the room. Once he had descended the stairs, I turned to Holmes, a look of shock evident on a face.

"It was never my intent to subject you to apoplexy, Watson," Holmes said. "However, Algernon North is the finest gentleman thief of whose acquaintance I have made in London. His willingness to help me in matters of this sort is one of the few reasons that I have not handed him over to the police."

I felt almost compelled to remind Holmes that the man was a criminal and he had duty to do so, but I knew Holmes too well. He would cite the fact that as a consulting detective operating outside of the law, he labored under no such obligation. I felt that it was best to simply let the matter drop. Reaching for my pipe, I lit it to steady my nerves and took my usual chair.

"What exactly do you plan to do next?"

"I intend to follow this new thread in the tangled skein which North has isolated for us," Holmes answered. "I had very much intended to spend the day here, but I am afraid that I shall have to go."

"Go? Go where?"

"First to Scotland Yard," Holmes answered. "Though the details of the theft at the Langham Hotel may not be public, I very much hope to persuade Gregson to let me know the facts in the case. And then, to the hotel itself. I shall, of course, have to go incognito."

So saying, Holmes rose from his chair and moved into his room. I heard him nosily open and close drawers, digging through the chaos which was his dresser and wardrobe. I moved to the window in order to take in a breath of fresh air when, peering down into the street, I caught sight of a familiar figure making his way towards our door.

"I rather think that you can save yourself a trip to Scotland Yard," I called to Holmes. "Tobias Gregson is calling on us now."

A moment later, the bell had rung below and Gregson was drawing into our sitting room.

"Were it not stuff and nonsense, inspector," Holmes said, "I should think that you were reading my mind. I was just on my way to pay you a visit."

"I have come in a professional capacity, Mr. Holmes. I, myself, did not think that you were needed, but Mrs. Hilda Devereux was quite insistent that you be made aware of what has happened."

"Good lord," I said, "has something befallen the Devereuxs?"

"Not exactly, doctor," Gregson replied. "Their home was burgled last night. A real slapdash job too. The front door was forced open. Mr. Devereux was sleeping in a chair in their parlor and was confronted by a man clothed entirely in black carrying what appeared to be a cudgel. The sight frightened the old man, but he emerged without so much as a scratch. As for the burglar, he got away scot free, and did not end up taking anything. In my own professional opinion, the burglar was not a professional. He was frightened by running into Mr. Devereux and left without even making a search for any valuables."

Holmes considered for a moment. "I do appreciate your coming, inspector. However, I do agree that you seem to be handling the situation. If it will be of any assistance to you, I can give you a description of the burglar."

"Good God man!" Gregson expostulated. "How could you possibly know?"

"Dr. Watson and I paid a visit on the Devereuxs last evening in connection with a case which we are currently investigating. While there, they told us an odd little story about how a young man had been taken ill in their sitting room earlier that afternoon, apparently struck down with heat stroke. As soon as I heard that story, my suspicions were aroused. In all probability, that young man is the burglar, described as being a young, fresh-faced man of about twenty-two or twenty-three years of age. That, I am afraid, does not narrow down a list of suspects for you, inspector, but it is, you will concede, a place to start."

"But why go through the pretense of pretending to suffer heat stroke if you were to simply burgle the house?" I asked.

"The theatrics of yesterday afternoon," Holmes said, "were merely a ruse for our burglar to familiarize himself with the layout of the Devereuxs home. I should wager that he had never stepped foot inside and needed to know the house's floorplan before he committed the actual act that night."

Tobias Gregson beamed. "A brilliant bit of work, Mr. Holmes. Truly brilliant."

Holmes waved his hand dismissively. "Save your compliments until I have done something really clever, Gregson. Now, while you are here, perhaps you can do me a favor and answer a few questions about the theft of a jewelry box which belonged to one Mrs. Arabella Hargreaves at the Langham Hotel."

"God almighty," Gregson exclaimed. "Mr. Holmes, you seem to know about everything, don't you?"

"Hardly," Holmes retorted coldly, "otherwise I wouldn't need to ask you about the details of the Langham Hotel case. Now then, inspector, what can you tell me?"

Inspector Tobias Gregson seemed, for an instant, to be at battle with himself. Could he divulge information to Sherlock Holmes, a man who had no true ties to the official police force? But Gregson knew as well as both Holmes and I that he had to. Though I am sure the inspector would have been loath to admit it, Sherlock Holmes was an invaluable asset to the Yard. From his inner breast pocket, the inspector withdrew a notebook and, flipping to the desired page, began to read from it.

"I'm afraid, Mr. Holmes, that there is precious little that I really can tell you. The job was obviously pulled by professionals. The jewelry case was a simple, unmarked box placed atop a bureau in the bedroom of the suite in which the Hargreaves were staying. It seemed obvious, therefore, that someone must have had knowledge of the jewels' whereabouts. Staff members of the Langham Hotel were questioned thoroughly, but they yielded nothing of consequence. I have had some of my men keep up-to-date on matters pertaining to the selling and cutting of diamonds on the black market, but that too has yielded nothing. In short, Mr. Holmes, the criminals came and went in the blink of an eye."

"It has been my experience, inspector, that domestic staffs are notoriously tight-lipped when it comes to interrogation. Nevertheless, I am sure that you acted as capably as you could under the circumstances. You have been of quite some use to me and now, I think it best that you return to the Devereuxs. Assure them that they need not be too concerned, but I would highly recommend that you post a constable outside the house for the time being."

"Do you anticipate further skullduggery?" Gregson asked as he rose to go.

"It is very possible," Holmes replied. "However, if I am correct, the job will be far less slipshod than it was. We are dealing with determined foes, inspector."

"Mr. Holmes," Gregson said as Holmes all but pushed him towards the door, "you seem to be onto something which I cannot very well divine. Just what exactly is going on here?"

"Do not concern yourself, inspector," Holmes curtly replied. "I shall make all known to you in short order. Good day to you."

Closing the door in Gregson's face, Holmes dashed back to his room. He emerged a quarter of an hour later dressed in simple workman's clothes. He was stooping, taking a number of inches off his stature and combed his usually neat hair into a wild coif. When he spoke he had affected a Cockney accent.

"Off to the Langham Hotel, Doctor," he said. "Here's hoping they take me on for the day."

I saw nothing of Holmes for the remainder of the day. I lounged about Baker Street enjoying pipeful after pipeful of my preferred Ship's tobacco. I casually perused the papers and continued the reading from the previous afternoon. As the afternoon was giving way to dusk, a light rain had descended over the city. I was just shutting up when I heard the street door open and Holmes bustled into the room.

"Expect a guest in fifteen minutes' time, Watson," Holmes said, scurrying to his own room. He called out to me as he dressed: "I made the acquaintance of a most amiable chap at the Langham Hotel today. His name is Giles Marker and he has been employed there for less than six months. We got to talking and when I pressed Marker for information about the hotel burglary, he shut up like a clam. However, I perceived in him a willingness to make money, no matter what he had to do to get it. So, when I offered him a few pounds if he stopped around at 221b Baker Street at precisely seven o'clock, I knew he would take it."

"What is this Giles Marker expecting exactly?" I asked.

Holmes swept into the room dressed in a clean, crisp shirt, waistcoat, and frockcoat. His remarkable ability to transform him into any character he chose was fantastic. The fact that he had completed this metamorphosis in reverse and restored himself to his usual character in the same amount of time was no less surprising.

"He is expecting to meet a man who would like to talk to him for a few moments. That, of course, is me. Do you have your service revolver handy?"

"Yes," I said. "Do you think that it shall be needed?"

"It is unlikely," Holmes said as he casually lit his pipe and tossed the extinguished match into the ashtray. "However, Giles Marker is a desperate man. I could read in his eyes that he was complicit in the Langham Hotel robbery and desperate men are liable to do the oddest things. Cold steel is a nice argument against desperate acts."

I reached into the drawer of my desk and withdrew my revolver. As I did so the bell rang below and I slipped the gun into my inner pocket. Holmes opened the door wide and called down into the foyer for our guest to come up at once. A moment later, a meek-looking man drew into the room. He was haggard in appearance, but I took that to be the result of a man who is on guard when faced with a situation which is simply too good to be true. Holmes introduced both himself and me before gesturing for Giles Marker to take a seat on the settee. Marker did so, fingering the brim of his bowler hat as he sat.

"Now then, Mr. Marker," Holmes said, "you can save both yourself and me a lot of trouble if you answer my questions as plainly and frankly as possible. If you do so – and I deem your responses satisfactory – I will recompense you for your time."

"I'll do whatever you ask," Giles Marker murmured.

"Excellent," Holmes smugly replied. He pulled on his pipe before asking bluntly, "What role did you play in the robbery at the Langham Hotel which occurred three weeks ago."

A sudden convulsion overtook the man's limbs as he jumped up from his seat. Seldom in my life have I seen a man run as Giles Marker ran across our room that evening. I dove for the door as he did and caught him by the sleeve. Marker struggled in my arms, flailing his outstretched arms in a desperate attempt to make a garb for the doorknob. I confess that he slipped through my grip and would have been through the door, out into the hallway, and down the steps had I not had the wherewithal to pull the revolver from my pocket. The metal caught the light in the room and Giles Marker's face became a mask of terror.

Turning on his heel, he rushed back the way he had come and I saw all at once that he was about to commit the most desperate of acts – he was making for the windows on the opposite side of the room. Holmes had already rushed to block his path and I too took to my heels in another bid to grab at the man's arms and subdue him. I caught him this time and, with all of the skill of the first-rate rugby player I was in my youth, brought the man down. I misjudged his distance from the pane of glass however, for I heard him make contact with it as he tumbled to the ground. Giles Marker went limp in my arms as I rolled off him. I stood and composed myself as Holmes knelt down beside the man, gnashing his teeth.

"I very much hope that you haven't killed our only lead, Watson," Holmes said sternly. I saw blood trickling down Giles Marker's forehead; a splotch of blood was also only too evident on the now broken windowpane. At length Holmes stood. "You have acted like an idiot, Watson," he said stingingly. "Luckily, the fellow is only out cold. Pour him a glass of brandy and we'll bring him 'round."

I did as Holmes demanded and, poured the drink down Marker's throat; he sputtered as he came to. I had now leveled the gun his direction in hopes that he would not attempt to make another break for the door or the window.

"Your desperation is palpable, Mr. Marker," Holmes sardonically intoned. "I could tell from the cloudiness of your eyes that you are a drug addict – and your actions this evening only furthered my suspicions. The promise of money only made you all the more on edge as you came here tonight."

Holmes slid into his chair. "Now then, Mr. Marker – the way you acted just now can very well be taken as the act of a guilty man. I very much doubt that it would take a jury of your peers to convict you of complicity in the theft had they seen what you did just now. So, I will give you a choice: you can either unburden yourself to me now and be let free, or you can remain as tight-lipped as you are and face possible time in gaol. The choice is yours."

Giles Marker drew in a deep breath. "There isn't much I can tell you," he said at length. "I was approached by a young chap. He called himself Turner, but I doubt that was his real name. He had been working at the hotel for only a few weeks so we bonded rather quickly as I'd only been working at the hotel for a few months. We both were working the floor where Mrs. Hargreaves was staying with her husband and, one evening, after work down at the pub, Turner told me he had this bright idea. He had seen Mrs. Hargreaves' jewels in her jewelry case and knew that he could make off with them easily. All he needed me to do was to make an impression of the key to the room and he'd split the loot with me.

"Well, I was hard up for money so I did as he said. It was easy as pie to make the impression of the key and hand it over to Turner. Then, one afternoon, Turner comes running down to the kitchens. He's got a bag tucked under his arm and he says that if anyone asks, I didn't see him. I knew exactly what he had done so I wasn't going to say nothing, sir. I wanted my cut of the money. Well, when the investigation started, I remained as quiet as ever about the whole blessed business. And then, something odd happened. I figured that Tuner was overplaying his hand by not coming back to work. Suspicion, I figured, would naturally fall on the man who disappeared the day the box was stolen. But no one seemed to worry about him. I even off-handedly mentioned him to one of the other footmen at the hotel and he didn't seem to know who Turner was.

"It occurred to me then that Turner had never really socialized with anyone else. I started to think that he was never really employed at the hotel and that he had only used me as an unwitting accomplice. My fears were confirmed a few weeks ago. You see, before he'd

41

pulled the job, Turner gave me an address and told me that that was the place to meet him to get my cut. I went and, to my horror, I found the place was an empty shop. Completely shut up like no one had ever had the place."

Sherlock Holmes considered for a moment. "This address," he said, "what was it?"

"I have it here," Giles Marker replied. Digging into the inner pocket of his coat, he withdrew a crumpled sheet of paper on which was scrawled an address I could not perceive. "I must admit," Marker continued, "when I met that friend of yours this afternoon, I got excited. He said that you would give me some money for a little job. As you can tell, sir, I have a bit of a pattern when it comes to offers which simply are too good to be true."

"You need not concern yourself now, Mr. Marker," Holmes said. He then added in his Cockney drawl: "Your coming here has made up for what you've done."

A look of astonishment and awe crossed Giles Marker's face as he now recognized Holmes as the man he spent the day with. "Bless my soul," he murmured.

From his pocket, Holmes withdrew a gold sovereign. "Not exactly the amount as promised, Marker," he said, "but I shall recompense you all-the-same. Be sure to spend it on something other than narcotics or alcohol. Now, run along!"

Given the opportunity to flee, Giles Marker rushed out of the room. Holmes settled into his chair, knitting his brow.

"Does this address mean nothing to you, Watson," he asked passing the sheet to me.

"I cannot say that it does," I replied, still sore from Holmes's cold words to me earlier. Those feelings were entirely lost when Holmes uttered:

"This address is directly behind Forbes and Sons Jewelry Shop."

I awoke the next morning to find that Holmes had already gone out. He had remained curiously silent the previous evening, and we had both retired to bed early. I set about busying myself for the day and trying my utmost to hide the broken windowpane from Mrs. Hudson for the time being. The hands on the clock were slowly creeping towards dusk and I still had had no communication from my friend when I received a telegram from him. He told me in no uncertain terms to meet him at the address of the empty shop which we had received the previous evening and to bring my revolver. No sooner did I receive his summons then did I clean my firearm, slip it into my jacket pocket, and set off for my rendezvous.

I instructed my cabbie to deposit me at the end of the road, and I cautiously made my way down the street, finding it curiously empty. Save for the lamplighter, who was applying a flame to the gas lamps which lined that particular boulevard, it appeared as though I was alone. I took a position across from the empty shop, ducking into the doorway of a similarly unoccupied building, and clicked open my watch. I cast a glance around for Holmes, but saw nothing. It was at that moment that the door behind me opened and I found myself almost tumbling backwards into the empty room. I felt a strong grip on my arm holding me upright and suddenly I found myself staring into Holmes's familiar countenance.

"What the devil are you doing in there?" I hissed.

"I am making the most of my surroundings," Holmes replied sardonically. Then, holding a finger to his lips, he pulled me into the empty shop and closed the door behind him. Much to my surprise, I found Inspector Tobias Gregson seated cross-legged on the floor before the glow of a candle.

"Perhaps," I said, "you wouldn't mind explaining just what is going on here?"

Holmes moved further into the room and took a seat opposite the inspector. From the folds of his light pea-coat, he withdrew his cigarette case. Proffering me one, I accepted, as he coaxed one out as well and lit it.

"I spent the majority of my day in this very room," Holmes began. "For members of the criminal classes in London, this stretch of road was perfect for their use. It is not heavily traversed and, as it sits directly behind a row of shops, one would not think that any illegal activity would transpire in so commonplace a locale. There has not been a great deal of activity here, but I would like to draw your attention, gentlemen, to the building itself for a moment. As you can clearly see, there is a row of windows on the second floor of that building. I would guarantee that there is a set of rooms up there where the proprietors of Forbes and Sons reside.

"However, I perceive that you both are very much in the dark about what is going on here, so allow me to elucidate. I believe that it was Poe who suggested that the best place to hide something was in plain sight. I knew from the start that a shop could not sell both imitation jewelry and the genuine articles, so my suspicion was aroused at once. I confess that the decision to begin investigating jewel thefts which occurred in the city in the past month was, at first, merely a shot in the dark. However, I knew that any sizable haul from a theft would have to be stowed somewhere or taken away to a third-party. Using my connections in the criminal fraternity, I learned that knowledge of the stolen jewels from the Langham Hotel was scarce. Obviously, no third-party was involved, so the thieves were still in possession of the jewels and were hiding out with them somewhere.

"And then I returned to that thought concerning hiding something in plain sight. Where else would one never suspect to find stolen jewelry: hidden among fake jewelry. I feel certain that Forbes and Sons was established as a shop to sell cheap, imitation jewelry to the sort of person like Kenneth Patterson; a young man with little true income who is on the lookout for a piece which could stand tall with the genuine article. This type of jewelry was the perfect camouflage for the stolen items. Seated alongside a very good imitation ring in a showcase was the perfect hiding place for a well sought-after, genuine ring."

"But, why on earth should they sell the ring if they were holding on to it?" I asked.

"Ah, to answer that question," Holmes continued, "we must analyze the make-up of the Forbes family. When I was not seated in this room today, I was carrying out a bit of reconnaissance work on the other street, peering into the shop windows of Forbes and Sons, trying my hardest to make out the characters inside. What I perceived were three young men: all could be described as fresh-faced youths between the ages of twenty-one and twenty-three."

"Exactly matching the young man who collapsed in front of the Devereuxs home," I interjected.

"And your description of the burglar," Gregson added.

"The three of them are the sons of Forbes and Sons," Holmes added, "and I noticed only two of them making use of the door to that empty shop across the way. Obviously, one of the sons was not part of the plan and unwittingly sold one of the genuine rings. When his brothers found out, they had to do all in their power to retrieve one of their stolen items. This went so far as consulting the ledger used at purchase to find Mrs. Devereux's address, and break into the house. Obviously, whoever masterminded the break-in at the Devereuxs house was not the same one who carried out the robbery at the Langham Hotel. The methods were totally dissimilar."

"But why should one member of the family be left out of the planning?" I asked.

"I am afraid that that is a question to which I have no answer, Watson," Holmes replied. "Familial distrust, I should imagine."

"But what do you intend to do next, Mr. Holmes?"

Holmes turned to the inspector. "I spoke with an associate of mine this afternoon. He informed me that, according to some of his own sources, the first whispers concerning the stolen Langham Hotel jewelry had begun to surface in the criminal underworld. It had begun to sound as if the thieves were going to make their move. I should imagine that the jewels will be cut and sent to the Continent this evening. Therefore, we are waiting until the moment is right to catch our men in the act."

No sooner had Holmes spoken did we hear footfalls on the pavement outside. Cautiously, we peered through the window and saw a man, dressed in a dark suit, and carrying a carpet bag in hand, approach the empty shop across the street. He knocked and, a moment later, the door opened and he stepped inside.

"Now is the moment, gentlemen," Holmes said. From the folds of his coat, he produced a revolver. I followed suit and we charged out of the shop and across the street. Whether our assault was the most well-judged strategy was a thought which I did not even have time to calculate. Holmes had kicked at the lock of the door and sent the hard piece of wall crashing through the frame. Pulling the hammer back on his revolver, Holmes disappeared into a dimly-lit passage. I charged ahead, listening to the shouts of confusion which emanated from the next room. Rushing in, I found the detective leveling his gun at three men: two of them I took be the fresh-faced Forbes boys and the third, holding what looked conspicuously like a diamond-cutting knife, I took be the hired diamond cutter.

"There is little point in putting up a struggle," Holmes said coldly. "I can tell – even from a distance – that you are all unarmed, save for that knife which is very much in my line of vision. You will find both of my associates and I are armed, making any attempt at an escape just as futile. I very much think that the game is up."

One day had elapsed and Holmes and I found ourselves seated comfortably back in Baker Street. We were, however, not alone as we both took in yet another warm, summer morning. Mr. Algernon North had taken a seat on the settee and was airily blowing rings of cigarette smoke about his head.

"I rather think, Sherlock," he said, "that you shall be owing me a favor now. If it weren't for me, you might have missed your men."

Sherlock Holmes blew a ring of smoke around his own head. Crushing his cigarette into the ashtray, Holmes leaned back in his chair. "I do admit that you played a central role in this drama, Algernon. But, who receives credit in this business is of little interest to me. The work is its own reward."

I cast a glance to the newspaper which sat folded in half on the table at Holmes's elbow. The headline proclaimed that the jewels stolen from the Langham Hotel had been recovered by the intrepid work of Inspector Tobias Gregson of Scotland Yard. I had seen Holmes peruse the paper earlier that morning and cast the periodical aside without as much as a word.

Algernon North snorted. "If someone had come along and taken the credit for one of my jobs," he began, "I think I would be put off by it all. But, that, I suppose, is where you and I are different, Sherlock."

North extinguished his own cigarette and stood. He picked up the imitation gold ring from the mantelpiece and scrutinized it once more under the gaze of his monocle. "Do you intend to add this to your museum of past successes?"

"Certainly," Holmes retorted. Taking the ring from North's hand, Holmes opened the drawer to his desk and tossed the ring into it. Algernon North rolled his eyes.

"Fine way to treat a piece of jewelry…even if it is fake."

Holmes returned to his seat and languidly crossed one leg over the other.

"One last question, old man," North said. "What about the genuine one? What did you do with that? Don't you expect that Mrs. Hargreaves will want it back?"

Holmes smirked. "I don't intend to pry that ring away from Miss Mary Devereux. It wouldn't do the couple any good. They seem quite happy about it. Besides, does one plain gold ring make any real difference?"

The Adventure of the Parisian Butcher

It has always been my intention to give the public as accurate and complete an account of my association with Mr. Sherlock Holmes; however, there have been innumerable times in our career together that I found myself having to alter facts such as names, dates, and places in order to relate matters of a sometimes scandalous or sensitive nature. On other occasions, I have found it necessary to hold back an account in its entirety; deciding as I laid my pen aside that it would be for the best that the particulars of some of Holmes's cases never be exposed at all. Such is the manuscript which follows: one of the few times when I determined it best that the document be consigned to some obscure corner of The Cox and Co. Bank vault never to see the light of day.

Sherlock Holmes was the very last of men ever to give credence to any sort of sixth sense, so it came as something of a surprise to me one rain-bedewed late summer morning when Holmes sat back in his chair and said: "I have the strongest intimation that something is wrong."

I set the paper down on my knee. "Whatever do you mean?" I asked.

Holmes passed me an open envelope. "That letter came to me last evening while we were away," he said. "It is, as you will doubtlessly notice, postmarked London. However, the writer of that letter is Monsieur Andre Dupont, a wealthy French businessman. Does the name strike your ear as familiar, Watson?"

"I cannot say with any certainty," I replied. "What does this Monsieur Dupont write to you about?"

"He does not say," Holmes replied, reaching for his cigarette case. "He was most irritatingly vague. However, he says that he will present himself at my rooms at eleven o'clock on the morrow – meaning, of course, today."

"Well, I don't see what makes you so particularly inclined to think that something is wrong."

Sherlock Holmes lit his cigarette and laid the burnt-out match in the ashtray at his side. "If you would do more than to observe the latest cricket scores in that very paper which you have currently splayed out across your lap, my dear fellow, you would find an article which announces that M. Andre Dupont will be arriving by the one o'clock boat from Paris as he is conducting some business with a few prominent English industrialists."

"Which means that Dupont has been in London for a day already?"

"At the least," Holmes replied. "Either M. Dupont had some business of a more illicit nature to attend to in the city, or he is very much in fear for his life. The fact that his arrival in the city has now been documented leads me to believe that he will have to go to some extremes to conceal his early arrival. By my estimation, a lookalike shall be disembarking from the one o'clock boat in M. Dupont's stead."

Holmes clicked open his fob watch. "It's nearly eleven now," he said. "If you would be so kind as to stay, Doctor. You could be of invaluable assistance."

I told Holmes that there was nothing that I would rather do than aid him in any way I could. No sooner had Holmes exclaimed: "Capital!" and clapped his hands zealously together did we hear the bell below chime. I could hear the sound of someone at the door conversing with Mrs. Hudson in the foyer and, a moment later, when our landlady drew into the sitting room, Holmes beamed at her.

"You may show M. Dupont up at once, Mrs. Hudson. His visit is not an unexpected one."

"I beg your pardon, Mr. Holmes, but it is not M. Dupont who is at the door."

Holmes knit his brow in confusion. "Who is it then?"

Mrs. Hudson produced our visitor's card and handed it to the detective. He read it, his face clouding further. Then, without a word, he gestured for her to bring the client in.

"Well," I said, once Mrs. Hudson had gone, "Who is it?"

"The card is most certainly that of M. Andre Dupont," Holmes said passing it to me. "But, as you will perceive, written upon it are the words: Alexandre – Valet."

"Why should Andre Dupont send his valet to you instead of coming himself?" I asked.

Holmes shrugged his shoulders. "I hope that the man shall endeavor to answer that very question."

Our landlady returned with a tall, lanky man in his early fifties. He was well-dressed, though I figured that the dark coat and bowler hat which he carried could not have been in the slightest comfortable, especially as the late summer weather had turned the atmosphere thick and cloying.

"I would not be incorrect in assuming that you have come on behalf of your master?" Holmes asked the servant.

"That is correct, sir," the man replied. He remained stiff as a board, totally unmoving as he spoke. "M. Dupont had all intentions of calling on you himself this morning, per his letter, but he decided otherwise at the very last moment. He would, however, be most grateful if you accompanied me to my master's home. He is still most anxious to speak with you."

"This business must be one of the utmost severity," Holmes said more to himself than anyone else in the room. "Very well. I shall come with you, provided that Dr. Watson is allowed to accompany me. He acts as my associate in all my cases."

The valet nodded his head slightly. His total lack of movement made the man appear to be some kind of statue. "That shall be quite alright, Mr. Holmes."

"Excellent! Then the doctor and I shall join you in the foyer in precisely three minutes."

Holmes quickly set out gathering up his things and, once we had made our way downstairs, we climbed into a waiting four-wheeler and soon found ourselves hurtling through the teeming streets of the metropolis.

"Tell me Alexandre," Holmes began, "how long have you been in M. Dupont's employ?"

"This autumn will be my fifteenth year."

"Would you describe your relationship with M. Dupont as a close one?"

"I should think that no man knows my master better than I," the valet replied.

"And you have no idea in the slightest what could be troubling him so?"

For a moment, a look of fear came into the valet's dull, grey eyes, before he said quite emphatically: "No, sir. I cannot think of anything."

I noticed the look and flashed Holmes quick glance. He locked eyes with me and I knew that he too had perceived the valet's clumsy attempt at deception.

Our cab drew up outside of a very well-appointed house tucked back behind a mighty oak tree which grew out of the well-manicured front lawn. The valet produced from his coat a ring of keys and, once inside, he divested us of our hats and led us into a large, open sitting room. The room was lined with expensive-looking oil paintings on three of its walls; the fourth taken up with a stylish set of French windows which looked out onto a neat stone veranda. At the furthermost end of the room was a large fireplace before which stood the man I took to be Andre Dupont. He was tall and lean – and not a day over forty – though he looked considerably younger, sporting an elegantly waxed mustache. He was well-dressed in an expensive black suit. He looked as if he were destined to be in that room; as though he were one of the subjects of the portraits on the wall that had come to life just to add flair to the space.

"Ah, Mr. Sherlock Holmes," he said, with the slightest trace of a French accent permeating his words, "thank goodness you have come."

"M. Dupont," said Holmes as he moved further into the room to shake hands with the man, "you need not be a detective to figure that you are quite distressed about something."

"I should imagine that my urgent letter and my subsequent behavior were enough to convey that to you."

"Indeed," Holmes said, "I have seldom encountered so curious a starting point to an investigation in my days as a consulting detective. Dr. Watson, my friend and colleague, can testify to that point."

I shook hands with Dupont and verified Holmes's words which seemed to put the aristocrat at some ease.

"I am in fear for my life, Mr. Holmes," Dupont replied. "Please, gentlemen, sit. I shall tell you the story through."

Dupont took a seat in a wingback chair while Holmes and I took seats on opposite ends of a plush-looking settee. After he had offered us cigarettes, Dupont leaned back in his chair.

"I am a wealthy man," he began. "As such, I have garnered a few *enemies* in my time. Business rivals have publicly threatened me, and I have more than once in my life avoided being brained by thrown rocks. I have developed a thick skin. However, petty threats and stones pale in comparison to the threatening letters which I have received in the past few weeks."

From his inner beast pocket, Dupont withdrew two envelopes. "The first," he continued, "was delivered to my home in Paris a week ago. At first I thought that it was yet another threat from a business rival; the message itself was short and quite vague: '*Your time on earth is running short.*' It was not until I examined the note more deeply did I truly begin to fear for my life. You see, Mr. Holmes, this message was written in blood."

I sat upright in my seat suddenly. Dupont passed the letter to my friend. He took it and observed it first with the naked eye before peering at it through his convex lens.

"It is genuinely blood," my friend said length. "You will doubtlessly recall, Watson, that when first we met I was in the midst of developing a test to determine whether a substance perceived to be blood is actually blood. The congealed quality of the substance is enough to tell me that it is not ink."

"Naturally, I was scared out of my wits," Dupont continued. "I made sure that all the doors and windows of my home were locked. I began to carry a gun on my person and slept with it under my pillow. My wife, Michelle, began to question me about my curious behavior; however I did not wish to disturb her.

"However, my genuine terror only increased when, shortly after the arrival of that first letter, my pet dog disappeared from outside my own home in Paris. I feared that he had run away, but after searching for little more than an hour, my staff and I discovered that it had been slain. My wife knew something was amiss and confronted me that very night. I showed her the letter which I had received and together we believed that it was for the best that we leave Paris. I did not wish to make public my intent to travel to London, but it somehow it ended up in the majority of both Parisian and British papers. It was for that reason that I plotted to arrive here in London a full two days before my public arrival this morning. We traveled with some of my most trusted staff so we should be wanting for nothing here in London. I even managed to hire a man with a similar resemblance to me to be seen leaving the ship publicly. I was taking no chances, whatsoever.

"I thought, Mr. Holmes, that I was safe. And then, yesterday morning, I received yet another letter. It is postmarked London."

He handed the second envelope to Holmes. The threatening message was, once again, terse and to the point: '*Death is Coming For You.*'

"It too," Dupont said grimly, "is written in blood."

He drew in a deep breath, attempting to calm himself. "Whoever has sent me these letters knew of my flight to London," Dupont continued. "*He* knew that I would leave early and has dogged my heels across the Channel. Mr. Holmes, I beg of you: please protect me."

"I am not a common bodyguard," Holmes retorted more coldly than I believed was warranted. He handed the letter back to our client, and eased back in his chair, crossing one long leg over the other in a deceptively languid manner. "I shall, however, do my utmost to help you in unmasking your antagonist. However, I must insist upon one thing M. Dupont: you must reveal to me all you know."

"I have told you everything."

"I do not think so," Holmes icily replied. "You identified the person stalking you as 'He' a moment ago, almost as though you know precisely who is responsible for these acts against you. If you gave me some indication of who this man might be, I can go a long way towards clapping irons about his wrists."

Andre Dupont sucked in another deep breath. "I know of only one man who would have cause to wish such misfortunate on me," he murmured. "But that man is dead. I am sure of it."

"Nevertheless, tell me about him M. Dupont."

Dupont leaned back in his chair and, for an instant, the ghost of a smile crossed his mouth. "You will notice," he began, "that I am a collector. These paintings on the walls are all originals. Are you an art enthusiast yourself, Mr. Holmes?"

"I can appreciate a Bond Street art gallery as well as the next," Holmes replied. I cast my friend a quizzical glance, silently asking him what this could possibly have to do with the matter at hand. Holmes met my eyes and seemed to silently address me saying that all would become clear in time.

"I have amassed something of a collection," Dupont continued, rising from his chair and moving to a small, elegant-looking bureau in the corner of the room. From his waistcoat pocket, he withdrew a key, and inserted it into the lock. He opened a cabinet door and removed a small case about six inches across, wrapped in a light cloth.

"I have always had a fascination with art," Dupont continued, "and from time to time, I have been captivated by the *oeuvre*. I confess that I have always been riveted by Bosch's depiction of Hell in *The Garden of Earthly Delights*. I suppose that is what led me on the path to having an eye for the fantastic and the *unique*."

Dupont accented the last word as he removed the cloth from the case. What lay beneath was a neat, glass container. It was the contents of that container which turned my blood to ice.

Within the case sat a neatly severed human hand.

Though I have a strong stomach and am immune to much, the sight made me feel dizzy for a moment. Perhaps it was the showman-like air which Dupont had adopted in revealing to us his unique piece of art. I looked to Holmes, but his face was cold and unreadable.

"Whose hand is this?" Holmes asked at length.

"The man's name was Jacques Bonnaire," Dupont replied. "He was a close friend of mine for many years until, after my wife and I had married, he attempted to make love to her. I caught him in the act and shot him on the spot. He was severely wounded and, as he lay bleeding, I told Michelle to call for the police at once. When she had gone, I must have lost my head, Mr. Holmes, for I took up a knife and cut off his hand. I just wanted to make a point to the blackguard not to cross paths with me anymore. The police arrived and dealt with the matter; luckily in France, crimes of passion are leniently treated under the law, and Bonnaire was hauled away to a hospital. I have not heard of him since, but I cannot imagine that he survived his wounds."

Sherlock Holmes remained silent. For once, I could read Holmes's cold, inscrutable eyes like a book and it came as little surprise to me when he opened his mouth a moment later and said:

"Frankly you disgust me, M. Dupont and I shall have nothing to do with you."

"But what about the threats to my life?"

"You seem like the type of man who is quite capable at defending himself," Holmes retorted. "And, should you be too much of a coward to face your threats, then do what cowards do best: *run*. You have shown yourself quite adept at that as well. Run away. Perhaps, back to Paris. Surely, Jacques Bonnaire will have quite a time crossing the Channel once again minus a hand and a bullet in his chest. That is my advice and I shall do nothing else but offer that alone. Good day, sir."

So saying, Holmes spun around on his heel and started out of the room.

When I managed to catch my friend, he was already standing outside hailing a hansom back to Baker Street. Once we were ensconced in the belly of the cab, I could see Holmes silently gnashing his teeth.

"It is said that you can judge a man's character by the company he keeps," he said "and I should surely never wish to keep company with M. Andre Dupont and his penchant for hacking off the hands of his rivals."

"I do not blame you, Holmes," I said comfortingly.

Holmes drew in a deep breath and sighed. "But I cannot help but think," he murmured, "that I may have been hasty in my judgment and I have sent a man to his death. I fear that if my intimations prove to be correct once again then M. Andre Dupont's death may very well weigh on my conscious."

Holmes refused to speak on the matter for the next few days and, it was only as I sorted through the first post of the day three days later, that the business of M. Andre Dupont reentered our lives.

"Postmarked Paris," I said as I held a letter aloft. I read the return address. "Inspector Durand. I say, Holmes, isn't that –"

"Yes," Holmes interjected. "Inspector Durand was the most competent of investigators who we ran across during that bad business at the Paris Opera House some years ago. Please, Watson, do me the service of reading the letter out."

I settled into my chair and opened the letter. It was written in an authoritative hand. It read:

Mr. Holmes,

You will no doubt remember my name well. Though we seldom worked side-by-side so many years ago, I considered it a pleasure to have seen you in action. You have developed something of a following here on the Continent as your name has begun to appear in the press quite frequently.

I wish then that it could be under better circumstances that I write to you, and I severely hope that when you receive this letter that you are able to drop whatever it is that currently occupies you and join me in Paris. To put it briefly, it is murder. The murder of Andre Dupont, the wealthy businessman. If it were only a routine investigation, I should not think of troubling you; however, the savagery with which this murder was committed is unlike anything I have seen in many years of working as a police inspector. Both M. Dupont and his wife, Michelle, fell victim to the murderer. They were both stabbed to death, and both were discovered with one of their hands neatly cut off.

"Good lord, Holmes!" I cried

The inspector's wounds seemed to cut into me like a knife as well and I felt a shiver run up and down my back. I hardly had time to register Holmes bolting from his chair and perusing the train directory.

"The boat-train to Paris leaves in two hours, Watson," he said. "If we make haste, we can still catch it."

"Don't you want to hear the rest of the letter?"

"On the train, Watson," Holmes said, as he rushed off to his room with a frenzied wave of his hand. "We must act while the game is still very much afoot."

The next hour disappeared in a flurry of packing of bags. Holmes rushed off a telegram replying to Durand and we soon found ourselves charging across the station platform and ducking into a first-class carriage. I was only catching my breath as the train became wreathed in smoke and pulled out the station. Once we found ourselves hurtling across the English countryside, I cast a glance across to my friend. He stared out of the window at the passing fields, his face betraying no discernable emotion. I wondered if the deaths of Dupont and his wife were, indeed, weighing on my friend's mind.

Knowing him, he would blame himself for their violent ends. I was almost inclined to say something to Holmes in an attempt to break him free from his reverie, but I decided against it.

We passed the voyage in relative silence, broken only by Holmes pressing me for more information from Durand's letter. After I had read a part through, he would sit in silence and contemplate the scant words for what masqueraded as hours before urging me for more.

Inspector Durand had explained that the room in which M. Dupont and his wife were discovered was the locked sitting room of their well-appointed abode on a well-to-do road in the middle of Paris. The bodies had been discovered by the valet, Alexandre, who had contacted the police at once. Aside from a servant girl, there were no other persons in the house.

A silent passage by boat was followed by another sojourn by train. It seemed as though the foul weather which had descended on London had followed us to the continent. Rain lashed the train compartment windows, and, when we finally arrived in Paris, we found ourselves rushing to hail a cab to avoid the deluge. Holmes had done us the service of booking us a last minute set of rooms at a hotel and, after we arrived, he sent off another telegram to Inspector Durand announcing our arrival. It had been a long, exhausting day and at the end of it I found myself famished. I ate a small repast, and was not surprised (though not pleased) that Holmes refused to take any nourishment. I had just gathered up my plates and silverware when we were arrested by a knock on our door.

Holmes answered the call and found the familiar figure of Inspector Durand in the doorway. The half-decade since last we had met had been good to the inspector. He was a tall, lean man, broad-shouldered and rather statuesque in appearance. He had a long face with deep-set eyes, and a shock of fair hair atop his head. Furling his umbrella, my friend relieved him of his coat and gestured for the representative of the Parisian police to draw up before the fire.

"You look as though you could use a drink, inspector," I said as I poured him a brandy from the sideboard. He accepted the libation all too readily.

"*Merci*, doctor," he said, draining his glass. "It has been quite a day."

Holmes took a seat opposite the inspector and lit a cigarette. "Dr. Watson did me the service of reading the details of the case," he began, "are there any particularities which you were unable to convey to me?"

"None, M. Holmes," Durand replied. "All of the facts which are in my possession were highlighted. And, alas, very little has been gained from the investigation."

"I assume that you have conducted an investigation of M. Dupont's papers and personal possessions?" Holmes asked.

"Why, of course," Durand said, appearing slightly injured by Holmes's question. Perhaps the inspector did not know Holmes well enough to know of my friend's low opinion of the official police.

"Did you happen to find any mention of a man called *Jacques Bonnaire*?"

Durand considered for a moment. "No," he said. "Why? Who is this Jacques Bonnaire?"

"At present," Holmes replied, blowing a ring of smoke about his gaunt head, "he is a suspect of particular interest. However, as it is a capital mistake to theorise before one is in possession of all the facts, I shall do my utmost not to let the lamented M. Bonnaire enter into the investigation at this time."

"But if he could have an impact on this case," Durand said, "it would be a grave miscarriage of justice not to pursue this particular thread. Who is Jacques Bonnaire?"

"Holmes and I were contacted by M. Dupont in London three days ago," I began. "Dupont had been receiving a number of threatening letters – first, here in Paris, and again in London. He believed that they were sent by a man named Jacques Bonnaire, his one-time friend who tried to seduce Dupont's wife. In retaliation, Dupont shot Bonnaire and cut off the man's hand. Dupont lost all traces of Bonnaire after the incident, but seeing how these murders have a strong link to the incident involving Bonnaire; it is understandable how he should become a suspect."

"I should think so!" the inspector exclaimed. "I shall make it a priority to look into this Jacques Bonnaire character."

"No, inspector," Holmes retorted rather coldly. "You should make it a priority to allow Dr. Watson and me to examine the bodies. I assume they have been taken to the mortuary? Excellent, though the hour is quite late, I can think of no time like the present to visit the morgue."

In short order, the three of us had donned our hats and coats and had stepped into the street. The deluge had lessened and a mist was falling upon us. Inspector Durand hailed us a cab and, as we climbed inside, a palpable silence descended over us. I watched as Holmes peered out of the cab at the rain-soaked city which passed by. The City of Light took on a haunting yellow glow as the undulating flames of gas lamps mingled with the wall of fog and mist into which our carriage trundled.

We alighted before a small, stone building tucked on a side-street. Inspector Durand eased open the street door and we stepped inside. The smell of death was overwhelming and I clapped a hand to my nose. Though I have in my time been in the presence of death and decay – as both a soldier and a doctor – I would never be able to become immune to the thick, cloying stench of loss. Holmes, however, did not seem to take notice and proceeded into the room. We approached two tables which stood side-by-side, the familiar shapes of cadavers atop them covered in a shroud.

Durand drew back the white sheets which covered the cadavers and I stared at their pale corpses. Holmes circled the table and, from his inner pocket, withdrew his convex lens. Leaning over the body of Andre Dupont, he held the lens close to the wound which had been the cause of his death. Moving swiftly to the body of Madame Dupont, he did the same. In life, Michelle Dupont would have been a lovely woman. She was tall and lean with a head of charcoal-black hair which would have cascaded down her shoulders. Despite what I knew of Dupont's dubious past, I could not reconcile the claiming of the life of someone who I was sure was guilty of nothing.

Holmes stood and pressed the magnifying glass into my hand. "I would appreciate a doctor's opinion," he said. "The wounds, they were inflicted with the same weapon?"

Approaching the bodies, I held the lens close to my eye and examined the wounds in much the same manner as Holmes had just done.

"These wounds were undoubtedly inflicted by the same hand with the same weapon," I said. "And, from the looks of it, I should think that the knife which did this was a large kitchen knife. The wounds are deep and quite wide."

"And the hands," Holms continued, "would you say that the same knife was used to sever the hands?"

"From what I could see, a different knife was used in this operation," I said after examining the bodies once more.

"A *different knife*?" Inspector Durand echoed.

"I should imagine that the weapon was not as sharp as the one which dealt death to M. Durand and his wife. The cut is far more jagged and less clean."

I returned the lens to Holmes who pocketed it wordlessly. He tapped his long index finger against his lips for a moment.

"Why should the murderer carry two knives on his person? What kind of butcher could have done this thing" Durand asked.

"I would be most surprised if the murderer chose to carry two weapons when one would be more than sufficient," Holmes replied. "A kitchen knife of the type which Watson described is a formidable weapon indeed."

"What exactly are you insinuating M. Holmes?" Durand asked.

Holmes smiled. "At the moment, nothing. I shouldn't wish to color your investigation more than I already have. The hour, I'm afraid, grows late and it has been an incredibly trying day for both the doctor and me. First thing on the morrow, however, I must make an examination of the murder scene. That can be arranged, inspector?"

"*Oui*, M. Holmes."

"Excellent," Sherlock Holmes replied turning sharply on his heel. "Then, Dr. Watson and I shall bid you farewell. Or, perhaps, *au revoir*."

We parted ways with the inspector in the street. Our carriage conveyed us back to our hotel where we silently made our way to our rooms. Once inside, Holmes divested himself of his coat and took up his briar pipe as he settled in before the fire.

"You are not retiring for the night?" I asked.

"No," my friend replied. "The cogs of my brain have been set into motion and I would be doing myself a disservice should I try to halt their natural processes this night. But, I am sure that you are exhausted my dear fellow, so you needn't wait up for me."

I began to undo my tie as I moved towards my room. I looked forward to a good night's sleep more than anything but, as I neared the open door, I stopped and turned around to address Holmes.

"You have begun to develop some theory, haven't you?"

Holmes blew out a ring of smoke which encircled his head. "I have," he replied. "If it is correct, I fear that this case may only grow ever darker."

I roused myself early the following morning only to find that Holmes was already awake. To my satisfaction I found that he was breaking his fast and, for a moment, I considered cajoling Mrs. Hudson into preparing French pastries at Baker Street if it meant that Holmes would take some sustenance more often. I joined him at the breakfast table and we exchanged pleasantries. I informed him that I had slept well, even after the grisly circumstances of the day, and was much relieved to hear that he too had made it to bed – albeit in the early hours of the morning. Holmes also informed me that he had sent an early morning telegram to rendezvous with Inspector Durand who would convey us to the home of the late Andre Dupont.

After we had finished, we gathered our things and made our way into the hotel lobby where we found the inspector standing at the ready for us. We exchanged a few words before we moved outside and into the awaiting cab. Though the rain had let up, the day was cloudy and foreboding. It did little to diminish the beauty of the city which, under the cover of darkness the night before, I had failed to truly appreciate. I have only been to Paris a handful of times in my life, but each time I have come away impressed by the splendor of such a lovely place.

Our carriage came to a stop on a picturesque road in the sixth Arrondissement of the city. As we climbed out, I cast a glance up the street and saw the great tower of the Abbey of Saint-Germain-des-Prés peering over the rooftops of the nearby buildings. Inspector Durand led us through a small garden, the vegetation of which did go some way towards tucking the house away from the street. He withdrew a key from his inner pocket and inserted it into the lock of the front door. He eased it open and we stepped through.

"I have done the utmost to keep the space just as it was when the bodies were discovered, M. Holmes."

"Your consideration is much appreciated, inspector," Holmes replied. "Your willingness to do so has already placed you above many of the inspectors at Scotland Yard. Now, can you show us to where the bodies were discovered?"

Durand led us through the foyer and into a well-appointed siting room. The room was small, surely not as grand as the room in which Dupont had entertained us in London, but a comfortable space nonetheless which clearly spoke to Dupont's obvious wealth. A set of French windows opened onto a small stone veranda, though I perceived that the glass had been shattered and the drapes undulated in the light breeze which circulated through the room.

"M. Dupont was found there," Durand indicated, pointing to a spot on the floor before the window. "His wife was found there by the settee. I have come to believe that the murderer forced his way in through the French windows and attacked M. Dupont. Madame Dupont was powerless to stop the murderer as she was trapped in the room."

Holmes stepped further into the room and I watched as he swiveled his head around like a great bird of prey peering through the underbrush. His piercing grey eyes scanned each opulent surface in the room. He turned quickly and, kneeling before the window, inspected the broken pane of glass. Holmes murmured inaudibly beneath his breath as he stood and then moved to the settee on the other side of the room. I watched him consider the space – the cogs in his brain almost visible through his eyes.

"You said that the valet, Alexandre, had discovered the bodies?"

"*Oui*. They were discovered late in the evening. M. Dupont, according to the valet, was in the habit of taking a nightcap and, calling on his master, he found the door to the sitting room locked. When M. Dupont did not respond to his knock, the valet forced the door down."

"And you said that there was no one else in the house at the time of the murder?"

"There was a maid, Jeanette."

"Did she have anything to add to Alexandre's story?"

"Nothing whatsoever, M. Holmes," Durand replied. "She said that she was in the kitchen at the time of the murder and heard nothing."

Holmes tapped his lips once more in contemplation. "I'd like to see the kitchen if you don't mind, inspector."

Holmes started out of the room before the officer had a chance to refuse. He exchanged looks with me, and I shrugged my shoulders. Holmes had seemed to have lost interest entirely in the room in which the murder had taken place. Judging by the size of the house, it was not surprising when Durand drew our attention to a door at the head of a narrow staircase. He led us down the set of steps and into the kitchen which was furnished with an extensive series of counters.

"M. Dupont had apparently given his staff leave when he left for London," Durand explained. "His unanticipated return meant that the number of the household staff was greatly diminished. As I understand it, the valet and the maid were the only ones in attendance, having accompanied their master to London and back again."

Holmes took a turn around the kitchen and, after he had performed what I could only imagine was the most cursory of examinations, he turned to us and declared:

"I should very much like to examine the veranda behind the house."

"There is a second set of stairs on the opposite end of the kitchen," Durand said indicating the spiral staircase which sat tucked in the corner.

"Excellent," Holmes cried. "Oh, I have forgotten my hat and stick upstairs. You gentlemen need not follow me back up. I shall return presently."

Holmes climbed the steps and I heard him move about upstairs. He rejoined us a moment later and, insisting that we use the servant's stairs, we made our way to the first floor of the house once more and, from there, out of the house and onto the small veranda.

Holmes took a turn around the veranda and once more stopped before the French windows. He examined a few shards of glass and then, standing, smiled as he clapped his arms behind his back and rocked ever so slightly from his heel to his toes.

"You seem quite pleased with yourself, M. Holmes," the inspector said.

"That is because I think that things are fitting together rather nicely," the detective replied. "However, I think the time has finally come for us to devote attention to Monsieur Jacques Bonnaire. I would very much appreciate it, inspector, if you did a little digging. Find out all you can about the man."

"I shall start at once."

"Excellent," Holmes beamed. "As for myself, I shall take a walk. Paris is a city with which I am not too intimate and I think that a perambulation will do me some good."

"Would you like me to accompany you, Holmes?" I asked.

"You needn't bother, Watson," Holmes replied. "You will find me silent company for the next few hours. Treat yourself, my dear fellow, to some of this city's more sumptuous delicacies. I know that *le petit dejeuner* to which we treated ourselves this morning will hardly be enough to satisfy your needs. Let us meet again in three hours' time at police headquarters. Will be that sufficient for you, inspector?"

Durand assured Holmes that it would be and we set off in separate directions. I figured that if Holmes were willing to lose himself in the city, then I should try to do the same. I walked aimlessly for some time until I came across a pleasant café. I stopped and enjoyed a cup of *café au lait* and a baguette which was quite to my liking. Wandering a bit farther afield, I soon decided that it was time for me to return to more familiar environs and, flagging down a cab, was conveyed back to our hotel.

As I sat alone in the carriage, I cast my mind back to the scene of the murder. Obviously Holmes had seen far more than either the inspector or me, but I could in no way put my finger on what it was.

What, I wondered, had he seen that helped him divine some connection with the mysterious Jacques Bonnaire whose name hung over this case like the grisly shadow of death? As usual, Holmes would not explain, and I wished that he would have shared with me his theory. He clearly saw some dark circumstances surrounding this already morose affair.

Deposited at the hotel, I spent the remainder of the afternoon in quiet contemplation and, I do confess, that I dozed off. I managed to rouse myself with time to spare and caught another carriage to the *Place Louis Lèpine*, home of the Paris Police Prefecture. The impressive grey stone building stared down at me as I made my way inside and, after asking for Inspector Durand, was told that I could find his office on the second floor. I ascended the staircase and walked down a corridor until I came to the inspector's small office and found him seated behind a cluttered desk; Sherlock Holmes seated across from him in the process of lighting a cigarette.

"Good of you to join us, Watson," Holmes said as I took a seat next to him. "Inspector Durand was just about to tell us what he has unearthed on Jacques Bonnaire."

I took a seat next to Holmes as the inspector opened a file which sat on his desk. "To begin," Durand said, "Bonnaire was the same age as Dupont. While Dupont was a self-made man, Bonnaire was born into his wealth. They would seem, then, to be at odds from the beginning, but from all accounts, the two were close friends.

"Bonnaire married a woman one year after Dupont married his wife. Bonnaire had two children – two girls – before the death of his wife after only a few years of marriage. Bonnaire's children were only six and eight years old respectively at the time of his *contretemps* with Andre Dupont nearly a decade ago.

"It appears as though the details of the incident as imparted to you, M. Holmes, by Dupont were accurate. Michelle Dupont did indeed contact the police at her husband's behest. The officer who answered the call, a man called August, has since left the force, but his report was easy enough to dig up. He says that when he arrived, Jacques Bonnaire lay on the floor of the master bedroom in a pool of blood. He clutched at his chest where he had sustained a bullet wound, his other arm at his side, minus a hand. Bonnaire was conducted immediately to a hospital. He was released after nearly two weeks and, since then, he has disappeared off of the face of the earth."

"No contact of any kind you say? No contact made with his solicitors or bankers?"

"*Non, M. Holmes.*"

"What of his children?"

The inspector turned a page in his file. "The eldest daughter severed all ties with the family and has gone to ground. I could find nothing on her whatsoever. The younger daughter – as we understand it – works at a cabaret, a well-known spot in the city called *Le Chat Noir.*"

Holmes leaned forward and crushed his cigarette into the ashtray perched on the edge of the inspector's desk. "She would make a most interesting study, inspector."

"You wish to speak to Bonnaire's daughter?"

"Of course," Holmes replied rising. "The sooner the better."

"We shall go tonight then, if it is your wish."

Holmes beamed. "Capital, inspector!" My friend clicked open his watch. "Ah, how the time has flown. I confess I find myself rather taken with your Parisian cuisine – and judging from the crumbs which Dr. Watson has yet to remove from his lapels, I should imagine that he is as well. I think you should dine with us, Inspector. We shall think no more of M. Bonnaire for the time being. I like to think that I am well-up on continental crime, but I cannot pass up an opportunity to discuss it with someone firsthand. I leave the choice of restaurant to you."

True to his words, Holmes refused to speak about the case for some time. Instead, we found ourselves seated before a sumptuous multi-course feast at an expensive Parisian restaurant within the hour. Holmes and the inspector discussed aspects of various cases which, I do confess, left me completely lost. I wondered if Holmes was purposefully distracting himself from the matter at hand. Perhaps, I reasoned, as I drained a glass of fine wine, he knew all too well the trials which lay ahead of us in the unraveling of this case. This matter had already taken a toll on my friend; in his mind he had failed his client, and now he was doing all in his power to bring the criminal to book, no matter how arduous the task might prove to be. I wondered just how close to the truth he actually was.

Night had descended when we quit the restaurant. The rain had continued to hold off and, still deep in conversation, Holmes insisted that we walk the rest of the way. Our perambulation was not a long way and we drew up outside of a very inauspicious-looking building. Stepping inside, I was at once struck by the loudness of the music and the cheers from the crowd. The room into which we stepped was wide and open, a stage situated at the furthermost end. Tables at which men and woman of all shapes, sizes, and apparent statuses, were distributed throughout the room and they looked on at the stage which was currently occupied by a group of women performing a dance which, I would imagine in London would have raised a decent number of eyebrows. Holmes, of course, took no notice and pressed on further into the room.

We took an empty table which was tucked away in the back of the barroom. The inspector and I followed Holmes's example as he sat, and in short order we were approached by a waiter. The detective ordered us a bottle of wine.

"Well, Holmes," I said trying to be heard in the loud room, "what exactly do you intend to do?"

Holmes smiled mischievously and put a long finger to his lips as the waiter returned to our table.

"*Parlez-vous anglais?*" Holmes asked the waiter.

Our man nodded politely. "*Oui, monsieur,*" he replied.

"Excellent," Holmes said. He stood and drew up a chair from a nearby unoccupied table. "Then I invite you to join us for a glass of this most excellent wine."

A confused look crossed the waiter's face and I am sure he was about to protest. However, Holmes all but forced the young man into the chair and had poured him a glass. Once the waiter had tentatively lifted the glass to his lips, the detective sat back in his chair.

"What is your name?"

"Henri, monsieur," the waiter replied. "Is there something I can do for you gentlemen?"

"I rather think that there is," Holmes replied. "My friends and I would like to speak with someone – one of the dancers, I believe. She would be about sixteen I should imagine. Her surname is *Bonnaire*. Does she sound familiar?"

Before the waiter had an opportunity to answer, a big man, dressed in a garish waistcoat sauntered up to the table. He was middle-aged, a head of orange hair peeping out from under the brim of a battered billycock hat. He held in between his large fingers a chewed-upon cigar. He addressed the waiter sternly in French before turning to us, cocking an eyebrow.

"I am the manager of this club, *messieurs*. Henri tells me that you want some kind of information?"

"We're looking for a young woman named Bonnaire," Holmes replied. "If you could help us find her, it would be much appreciated."

Holmes coyly removed a coin from his inner pocket and slid it along the table. The glint caught the man's eye immediately and he picked it up, stowing it away as though he feared immediate robbery.

"I know precisely of whom you speak," the manager replied.

"We would like to speak with her at once," Holmes said. "It is imperative that we speak with her this evening."

"I shall take you to her," the manager replied standing.

Holmes cast the inspector and I a beaming grin as the manager led us through the labyrinth of tables and chairs. Moving past the patrons of the club, we made our way to a small door which communicated with the backstage. The dimly lit, private portions of the theater were alive with energy as dancers rushed hither and thither and stagehands worked to lift and lower curtains and drops. I caught sight of Holmes casting a glance over the theatrical mechanisms before we were urged along by our guide.

"The *mademoiselle* you seek has not gone by the name Bonnaire in some time," the manager said, "but there are few girls working here who are quite so young."

I felt a sudden feeling of reprehension for the man. Having seen the risqué nature of some of the routines performed in this place, I couldn't imagine a mere adolescent being involved.

We came to a door which, I concluded, led into the ladies' dressing room. The manager addressed one of the dancers about to enter and, after she disappeared, he informed us that she would fetch the young lady we sought. The dancer was true to her word and emerged from the dressing room a moment later with a petit girl in toe. She was young – Holmes's estimation of about sixteen or seventeen seemed most accurate – but she had quite a pretty countenance which, enhanced with the elaborate makeup utilized in the cabaret, did give the girl something of a salacious appearance. She looked at the three of us and arched an eyebrow. Holmes asked if the girl spoke English to which she nodded.

"*Mademoiselle*," Holmes began, "my name is Sherlock Holmes, this is friend and associate Dr. John Watson, and this is Inspector Erique Durand of the Paris Police Prefecture. You are the daughter of Jacques Bonnaire, are you not?"

The girl drew in a deep breath. "That is not a name I have heard in almost a decade, sir."

"Mademoiselle," Holmes continued, "we have reason to believe that your father is very much alive and responsible for the murder of Andre Dupont and his wife. It is most important that we speak to you at once."

Her eyes darted around the crowded backstage area. "Allow me a few moments, gentlemen," she said softly. She darted back into the dressing room and emerged again a moment later, a cloak draped about her shoulders. She then led us out of the building and into a narrow alleyway behind the theater.

"I apologize for the quality of the space," she said, "but we can speak privately here. I come here to think often and, I do confess, my father is often in my thoughts."

"Naturally," I said, laying a reassuring hand on the girl's shoulder. "What is your name?"

"Emma," the girl replied. "Though, most of the girls around here just call me Em. No one has called me Mademoiselle Bonnaire in quite some time. You say that my father is implicated in the murder of M. Dupont?"

"That is correct, Mademoiselle," Durand said. "You have not heard from your father recently, have you?"

"*Non*," Emma Bonnaire replied. "I do not think that I would want to after what happened."

"Perhaps," Holmes said, "you ought to explain."

"My father and my sister were the only things in my world after my mother died," Emma said. "We were a close-knit family. My father was kind, decent man. However, he – like so many – took to drink as a way to cope with the death of his wife. He soon could only take solace in the bottom of a bottle and, in his fits, he was quite uncontrollable. He was a big man, gentleman. And strong. Once, I found him seated alone in our sitting room, clutching an empty bottle. He saw me and flew into a rage and grabbed me by the arm. He very nearly pulled my arm from its socket.

"I was too young to notice it, but I suppose my father was rather keen on Madame Dupont. She was a handsome lady, I will admit and, in one of his drunken rages, I can only imagine what went through his mind but I cannot defend what M. Dupont did, gentlemen. It was wrong and…*savage*. I never thought that a man could stoop so low. It was not simply enough to shoot my father, but he went and cut off his hand too."

Emma Bonnaire held back a choked sob. I proffered my handkerchief which she accepted as she dabbed at her eyes. "*Merci, monsieur le docteur.*

"I can recall visiting my father in the hospital with my sister," she continued after a moment. "He was barely conscious and in a great deal of pain. I could read the look of disgust on my sister's face. She felt not pity for the prostrate figure laid out before her, but anger -- anger that he would attempt to seduce another man's wife and get caught in circumstances such as these.

"I suppose it came as little surprise to me then that she ran away shortly thereafter. It was one of the hardest things I have ever had to experience in my short life. It was made all the worse when, after I learned that my father had been released from the hospital, he did nothing to reclaim me. I was subsequently entrusted into the care of an orphanage where I remained for some considerable time. I would often lie awake at nights just contemplating my loneliness, gentlemen. That was until I decided to strike out on my own and join this cabaret. It has served as a home for me. Hardly an ideal one, but a shelter – and a family – nonetheless."

My heart simply broke for young Emma Bonnaire and I laid another reassuring hand on her shoulder. She cast a glance up at me and her eyes looked like shattered mirrors. She pressed the handkerchief back into my hand and drew in another deep breath.

"Mademoiselle Bonnaire," Holmes said at length, "while you may not have heard from your sister or your father, can you think of anything unusual happening to you within the past few weeks?"

"I can think of nothing," she replied, "aside from, perhaps, the man who loiters outside the theater, but I cannot imagine how that could have any connection to this."

"Humor me if you please, Mademoiselle," Holmes continued. "Who is this man who loiters outside the theater?"

"I have never seen him clearly," Emma Bonnaire replied, "but he has become something of a legend amongst the girls and me. One of my friends, another dancer, named Suzette, said that one night after a show she was exiting the theater through this very door here and was making her way up the alley when she heard someone moving about behind her. She turned and saw the outline of a man standing just over there."

Emma Bonnaire pointed to a spot beyond Holmes and the inspector at the foot of a small set of steps which led down into the alleyway.

"Suzette said that she could not quite make out his face, but he appeared to be an old man. He was hunched over and seemed to have some difficulty in breathing. It was quiet night, Suzette said, and she heard his raspy breath as he leaned on the staircase railing. Suzette was about to go and ask him if he needed a hand, but she said that fear overtook her. You gentlemen have certainly heard tales of defenseless women in alleyways in the early hours of the morning. That nightmare scenario running through her head, Suzette turned sharply and ran out of the alleyway.

"The next day, she told us about him and cautioned us to be on our guard. We heard and saw nothing of the mysterious man in the days which followed. However, one Friday evening a few weeks ago, a few of the girls and I decided to celebrate the end of the week. We all left together and were making our way of the theater when we caught sight of him standing at the head of the alleyway. He was a tall, gangly-looking man dressed in a shabby, oversized coat. His hair was long and tumbled about his shoulders. And his beard was lengthy and dirty-looking as well. So shocked were we by his sudden materialization at the end of the alley that we all turned and raced back inside the theater.

"Since that day, gentlemen, we have heard nothing from the man. We have taken him simply to be one of the less fortunate who is forced to seek refuge on the streets. I very much fear that our minds ran away with ourselves and made a demon out of this man."

The faintest ghost of a smile seemed to play upon Holmes's usually cruel, thin lips. "Mademoiselle Bonnaire," he said, "I cannot thank you enough for your invaluable assistance."

From his pocket, the detective withdrew a few francs and pressed them into the girl's hand. "If these can be of any help to you, mademoiselle, please take them."

Then turning to us, he added: "Come gentlemen, I very much suspect that – despite the lateness of the hour – the night is still young for us."

We bade Emma Bonnaire farewell and walked to the end of the alleyway and into the street.

"Well, M. Holmes," Inspector Durand said, "what do you intend to do next?"

"Part ways for the time being. I should very much like it if you could supply me with a city map, inspector. If you could annotate it, as well, showing any spots in the city where you know there to be a large homeless population, I would find it of great assistance. Let us all meet then once more at our hotel in an hour's time?"

Extending his arm, Holmes hailed a cab and I clambered inside after him leaving Inspector Durand on the street with a look of stupefaction etched on his face.

Once we were within the cab, Holmes turned to me, and solemnly asked: "You did remember to bring your service revolver?"

"Of that you can certain," I replied.

"Excellent. I very much suspect that we shall be in need of it tonight."

True to his word, Inspector Durand met with Holmes and me again at our hotel. He produced from the valise which he carried a map of Paris which he spread out on the dining table.

"In an attempt to answer your question, M. Holmes," Durand said, "I consulted with a few of my fellow officers. They all agreed that here is the place where most of the city's poor some to congregate."

He pointed to a spot on the map along the River Seine. "The place is something of a colony," Durand added. "They live along the river and under bridges."

"Excellent," Holmes said. "Then that is where we are headed now."

Holmes moved to the door and pulled on his hat and coat. "It has begun to rain, so take proper precautions. Now, come along."

Silently we made our way outside and into a tumultuous deluge. It was quite a feat in tracking down a cab and I fear that I was soaked to the skin by the time that we three sat ensconced in the relative warmth and comfort of a carriage.

Chilled from both the wet and the anticipation and suspense that I was being kept in, I very nearly exploded once we found ourselves rattling through the deluge.

"What are we doing, Holmes? I am used to your characteristically dramatic behavior, but this is beginning to be a bit much."

Holmes replied in his usual, cool tone: "We are going to confront Jacques Bonnaire."

A shiver ran up and down my spine – a chill which I cannot fully attribute to the rain which had seeped into my clothes.

In short order, our carriage eased to a halt. Holmes gestured for Inspector Durand to lead the way and, alighting, we rushed out of the carriage, seeking shelter beneath the inspector's umbrella. We stood on a bridge overlooking both the River Seine as well as a stone walkway which ran parallel to the river. Durand informed us that the most likely place for us to find the homeless community was directly under the bridge. Locating a set of stone steps, Holmes pressed on undeterred.

In the darkness and rain which lashed at me, I lost sight of Holmes. I followed close at the inspector's heels, but it felt as if we were headed into some black void; the waters of the Seine looking indistinguishable from the inky darkness which surrounded us. Standing, disoriented and shivering in the pouring rain, it was something of a godsend when I felt myself run into Holmes. He pressed a finger to his lips and, from the folds of his coat, withdrew a bulls-eye lantern. I sheltered my friend's hands from the rain as he struck a match and let the single point of yellow light pierce through the night.

"Now, follow me, gentlemen," Holmes whispered, "and, pray, keep silent. If he thinks that we are searching for him, then I'm afraid that the bird shall fly the coop."

We turned together as a small herd under the bridge and into the darkness; the pinpoint of light acting as our guide. I perceived, even in the dark, what speared to be outlines of people shuffling in the night. Just as both Holmes and the inspector had suspected, we were soon surrounded by an assortment of the city's beggars and vagabonds. I have witnessed much strife in my lifetime, but I felt additional pity to see such a concentration of sorrowful beings.

As we moved on, passing one knot of people each sprawled out on the cold stone, sleeping huddled under makeshift blankets or wrapped in their tattered coats, Holmes stopped suddenly and shone the lamplight on a tall, rail-thin specimen who lay before us. Even in the dark, I could make out something familiar about the man. Though I had never clapped eyes on him, I knew at once that this must be the mysterious apparition who seemed to haunt *Le Chat Noir*.

The creature was some kind of nightmarish vision. He was a tall, thin man, almost to the point of emaciation. His gaunt face was shrouded, however, by an unruly, unkempt beard, and a mangy, tousled head of long hair cascaded about his face. He was clad in a shapeless brown overcoat, done over in patches and stitched back together as though someone had tried to save it from the precipice of death itself.

Holmes whispered two, haunting words: "Jacques Bonnaire."

Movement came to the man's limbs and he opened one, bloodshot eye, wincing in the light.

"*Qui tu es?*" I heard the man rasp against the wind and rain. Despite my limited knowledge of the French language, I knew that the man was asking us who we were.

"My name will mean nothing to you," Holmes replied, "but this is Inspector Durand of the Paris Police Prefecture and we have come to arrest you for the murder of M. Andre Dupont and his wife."

It is beyond my skills as a writer to attempt to describe the look of savagery which crossed the man's face at these words. In an instant, the pity for the poor soul who lay before us melted away as he transformed into some uncontrollable beast. I watched, helpless with horror, as he dug into his inner pocket and withdrew a long knife. I caught a glimpse of his shirtsleeve dangling about where his one hand once resided. With what I can only imagine was all of the man's limited strength, he hauled himself up from the ground and attempted an escape. So startled were we by the sudden convulsion which had overcome Bonnaire that Holmes, the Inspector, and I completely failed to stop him. Time seemed to slow to a crawl before Holmes cried out:

"Quickly! Cut him off on the other side!"

I took to my heels and returned the way we had come and I soon found myself sprinting along the stone causeway which ran along the river. The rain had reduced the stones into something as slippery as ice and I almost lost my footing on several occasions. I could barely make out the scene which transpired beneath the bridge, but with little else place to go, I stood my ground and pulled the hammer back on my revolver. I aimed, not hesitating to shoot at whatever leapt out at from the darkness.

I heard the sound of Holmes's voice calling through the night and I momentarily lowered my gun for fear that I might strike my friend on accident. No sooner had I done so then the figure of Jacques Bonnaire flew out at me from the void. His face contorted into some satanic visage, he screamed like a banshee as the knife flashed in the air and I let out a gasp as its point caught my coat sleeve. I felt the cold steel against my flesh followed by a moment of intense, searing pain as though I'd been struck by a red hot poker. I dropped my gun and pressed a hand to my wound. The man seemed to have lost interest in me entirely, however, for he turned and started to run along the way I just come. I saw him raise the knife high over his head once again in search of either Holmes or Durand.

In one swift movement, I had gathered up the gun from the ground, and squeezed the trigger. The explosion sounded tremendous in the relative quiet of the early morning. The bullet met its mark in the back of Jacques Bonnaire and I watched as he tumbled to the ground, his weapon falling from his hand.

A second later, I felt a hand on my shoulder and looking up, I found myself staring at Holmes.

"Tell me that you are not hurt, Watson," he said.

He shined the light over my arm and I caught sight of a gash running along my forearm, but I was numb to the pain. The terror which had surged through my body had yet to let go of me.

"Jacques Bonnaire," I said breathlessly, "is dead."

That was the last I recall before total darkness overwhelmed me.

When I came to, I was seated upright in my bed in the hotel. Sherlock Holmes and Inspector Durand sat on two chairs at the foot of the bed keeping vigil. I smiled as I came to and made to reach for my watch, only to find that my arm had been wrapped in a sling.

"It's barely five in the morning, Watson," Sherlock Holmes said.

"I haven't felt this bad since the war," I joked. My jest drew a smile from both men.

"Your wound was a superficial one," Durand said. "M. Holmes insisted that we get it dressed and our physician at the prefecture insisted that we have it attended to…as you can see."

"A bloodletting was worth it, I should think," I said, "if we were able to apprehend Jacques Bonnaire and bring an end to this business."

"I rather think not," Holmes replied darkly.

At these words, the inspector and I both turned to face Holmes; our mouths agape.

"M. Holmes, what are you talking about? Jacques Bonnaire attacked both you and Dr. Watson in his attempt to flee from the police. He was carrying a knife which, I am told, matched the type which was used to sever the hands of M. Dupont and his wife. Are you insinuating that he was innocent all along?"

"Nothing of the kind, inspector," Holmes replied, crossing one leg over the other. "In fact, it was Jacques Bonnaire who did sever the hands of the deceased. But it was *not* Bonnaire who killed M. Dupont and his wife."

"Well then, who is guilty?" I sputtered.

"Bonnaire's eldest daughter," Holmes replied. "You, inspector, will know her better as Jeanette the maid."

"*Mon dieu*," Durand said. "M. Holmes, I think you ought to explain yourself."

"Gladly," the detective said, as he lit a cigarette. "From the outset of this business, I figured that there was more to the case. M. Dupont showed me two letters which were making threats against his life. The second of these was postmarked London which meant that whoever sent it had to have been in the city and returned just as quickly when Dupont and his wife decided to flee. Now, ask yourself one question, inspector: Jacques Bonnaire -- a man who is minus one hand and who has been inflicted with a near fatal bullet wound – do you suppose he would be capable of crossing the Channel as quickly as he did in his condition? What's more, you and I both saw how destitute he was. The man was living on the streets and would surely not have been able to pay the fare for two consecutive trips, let alone one.

"Knowing that there was a conspirator involved in this affair was only made all the more plausible when I was struck by the presence of two different knife wounds upon the bodies. You yourself asked the question, inspector, why should the murderer carry two different knives when one would be more than sufficient? The simplest answer is that there was more than one murderer involved. And, this became even more likely after an examination of the scene. You will doubtlessly recall that I took a moment to analyze a few shards of glass which I found on the veranda. You assumed that that glass was left after the murderer gained forceful entry into the house. If that had been the case, inspector, the glass would have been found on the inside of the room and not outside. That window was broken *after* the murders were committed.

"And, lastly, you told me, inspector that the maid, Jeanette, was in the kitchen and heard nothing the night of the murder. Perhaps you would be so good as to cast your minds back to the afternoon we examined the scene. I returned to the room to fetch my hat and stick – "

"And I clearly heard you moving about upstairs," I interjected.

"As I figured that you would," Holmes replied. "Jeanette would have to have been lying when she said that she could not hear anything transpiring upstairs. The design of the house and the kitchen would have placed her almost directly underneath of the room in which her employers were killed. The weapon itself is also connected with the kitchen. It would not be too difficult a task to search the kitchen for a missing knife, inspector. But, if you should discover one feel free to send it my way. I have developed something of a test which will differentiate blood from a whole host of other substances. Its presence on a blade should not be too difficult a thing to ascertain given a few hours of concentration.

"As I see it, Jeannette – if her name truly is Jeannette – felt not repulsion for her father when she saw him lying, dying in a hospital bed all those years ago, but a yearning for revenge against the man who had done this. Her disappearance gave her ample opportunity to begin seeking employment in some of the most wealthy houses in France, bringing her into the social circle of M. Andre Dupont. After some years, I rather think that Dupont would fail to recognize the little girl who had once been the daughter of his friend, and hired Jeannette, completely unaware of the conspiracy against him. Jeannette was working with her father to avenge him and began the persecution creating fear in the Dupont household. Even when he attempted to flee, she would follow. Dupont told us that he brought only his most trusted staff to England, and you confirmed, inspector, that Jeannette was in London when we investigated the scene of the murder.

"On the night of the murder, Jeannette aided her father's entry into the house. She stabbed to death both M. Dupont and his wife before her father began his bloody task. Once she had managed his escape, Jeannette broke the window to convincingly approximate a break-in – casting suspicion on someone outside the house – and then returned to the kitchen. I am glad only that the police investigation has run this long, Inspector. Should Jeannette have tried to flee before now, surely she would be easily traced. However, I suggest that you apprehend her as soon as possible. News of the action by the river shall spread fast and, with nothing else to lose, I fear that she shall do something drastic in so desperate a situation."

Durand rose from his chair. "I shall put my best men to it immediately."

"Excellent," Holmes replied. The two shook hands.

"It has been an absolute pleasure working alongside you on two separate occasions and, should the needs arise, please feel free to contact me again."

"I shall do so only too happily," Durand replied. "I shall see myself off. *Au revoir*, gentlemen."

I found myself feeling in much better sorts during the remainder of the day, and the following morning, Holmes and I found ourselves once more trundling across the French countryside by train. Holmes had remained silent about the case but, as he sat, casting a glance out of the yet again rain-streaked windows, I noticed a certain melancholia descend upon him.

"You have vindicated yourself," I said trying to coax him from his brown study. "You have seen justice served once again."

"You are right, Watson," Holmes replied, "but one cannot go unaffected by what we have witnessed here these past few days. This adventure of the Parisian Butcher has only reinforced to me what a bleak world we inhabit, Watson."

"Well," I said, "it should reinforce what a role you must play in it, then. If the world is as bleak and dark as you make it out to be, then surely the world needs a Sherlock Holmes to maintain the light."

The Adventure of the
Burning Man

One morning in the autumn of 1885; a grey, sodden day plagued by a heavy rain, I looked up from my newspaper at the breakfast table to see Sherlock Holmes all but throw his violin onto his chemical workbench. He tossed himself into his chair before the fire and heaved a heavy sigh, casting a forlorn look out the rain-streaked windows. I knew at once what had brought about my friend's melancholia: since our sojourn to Paris nearly two months earlier (a case I have drawn up for my own reference, but I fear is too ghastly to put before the public), Holmes had complained of a lack of truly challenging cases. The ones which he had dealt with in the past weeks – though completed satisfactorily – had failed to enthrall him and turn the cogs in his brain. And there was little which Sherlock Holmes detested more than the routine.

I tossed the paper down finding it too difficult to deal with Holmes's foul mood and digest the most recent news from the Mahdist War. The papers were reporting the most recent developments and, though I felt that it was my duty as a former military man to keep myself abreast of the conflict, I was still too haunted by my time in Afghanistan to read much into it. I crossed to my chair and coaxed a cigarette from its case and settled into my usual seat. Holmes, slumped low across from me with his head to his breast looked like a defeated man. I resisted the urge to roll my eyes at Holmes's frankly petulant behavior. Though I was in awe of Holmes, there were times – especially in the early days of our partnership – that I found him to be intolerable. I daresay that in his black moods, my friend regarded me with a certain degree of derision. Thusly disposed, it became a matter of inveigling him out of his morose disposition, a task which was much easier said than done.

"What you were *attempting* to play," said I, emphasizing the cruel way in which Holmes had treated his musical instrument, "I don't think I've heard it before. You are composing?"

"It's best to do something in order to stave off idleness," Holmes rebuked. "I fear that I am failing."

Holmes reached for his pipe and began to fill it with tobacco from the Persian slipper. The forceful manner in which he did so once more betrayed his palpable frustration with his current position. Applying a match, Holmes sat back in his chair, attempting to lose himself in the thin rings of smoke which curled about his gaunt head, but instead he turned to me and said:

"It is no mean feat to discern that you are frustrated with the recent developments concerning the conflict in Africa."

"You refer, no doubt, to that newspaper article I was reading this morning?"

"Precisely," Holmes replied. "You seemed, despite the regular glances in my direction as I tried to occupy myself with the violin, to be furrowing your brow as you read. Only moments ago you tossed the thing down entirely. Are the developments bad ones?"

"I cannot say with certainty," I replied. "Though I may have appeared to have been concentrating on it, I really have not had the heart to engage much with the reports. My constitution is still suffering from the strain of the Afghan campaign. Further reading on British colonialism in Africa is too much. It brings back certain *memories*."

I need not delve into the horrors which I witnessed as a medical doctor during my time in both India and Afghanistan. Suffice it to say, there were still times – even years after I returned from the East – that I would awake with a cold sweat running down my brow, the things I witnessed still very much engrained in my mind.

"The saying is correct, then," Sherlock Holmes said drawing me back from my reverie, "'the sun never sets on the British Empire.'" He drew on his pipe. "Do you, doctor, think it a worthwhile venture?"

I arched an eyebrow, caught off guard by a question which was extremely out of character for my friend to pose to me. I stammered for a moment looking for the best place to begin answering such a complex question, when the bell rang below. Holmes sat upright in his chair, the prospect of a client on our stoop having already banished any interest in holding a discussion on the merits of colonialism.

We heard Mrs. Hudson answer the call below and, straining to make out the voice of our caller, I looked to Holmes as he eased back in his chair, a look of some dejection crossing his sharp features.

"I detect the familiar tread of Tobias Gregson on the stair," he said. It was clear that Holmes had hoped for an outsider; someone come with a desperate plea for help. To Holmes's mind, the police only came to him when they were out of their depth which, he figured, was their natural state and, as a result, the cases which were presented to him by members of the Metropolitan Police were of a simple, unsatisfying nature.

Before Gregson could even knock, Holmes called out his name and the inspector drew into the room with a bemused smile on his face.

"Your gait is a tell-tale indicator of your presence, inspector," Holmes said. "Nevertheless, you look soaked to the skin and, I should wager that your journey by train was a restless one. Draw up before the fire and tell me what exactly has brought you to my door."

Tobias Gregson took a seat on the settee, having relieved himself of a wet ulster. I saw him stop and peer down at the tossed aside copy of *The Times* which had very nearly been the topic of conversation.

"I should have figured that your house, Mr. Holmes, would be the one in all of England where I could escape from news on the

Mahdist War," Gregson said leaning forward and reaching his hands out towards the flame. "I thought you tried to not clutter your brain with such things."

Holmes replied. "It was Dr. Watson who was perusing the article to which you refer. You are nevertheless right, Gregson: I do try to keep myself free of such trivial matters. I cannot imagine that your business has much to do with that international conflict, so pray proceed."

Tobias Gregson laughed. "Well, there I'm afraid you're wrong, Mr. Holmes. The problem which brings me to you today is indirectly connected with that business in Africa. But, before I begin, I really ought to ask how you knew that I traveled by train this morning. I should know your methods by now, but I cannot help but be impressed whenever you give such an off-handed demonstration as that."

"Your coat was wrinkled," Holmes said, "no doubt from your attempts to sleep in your compartment. You must have come directly from the station, for wrinkles like that are not easily made in a hansom cab. The earliness of the hour seemed to confirm to my mind that you had traveled all night. I need not speak to the lack of comfortability in a train carriage."

Gregson laughed. "As always I think that you have done something clever."

"If I were looking for amusement," Holmes said, "I would say that what I have done is clever, but the explanation robs it of all excitement. I have had this very same conversation with Dr. Watson on a number of occasions: it is not difficult to construct a series of insinuations, each supported by its predecessor and, if presented with the starting point and conclusion alone, a rather startling effect is produced. However, this is all discourse for another time and place. Pray, lay the facts of your case before me, inspector, and omit nothing at all."

Gregson drew himself up and removed a small notebook from his inner breast pocket. Holmes sat back in his chair, steepling his fingers in his habitual manner of contemplation.

"As you deduced, Mr. Holmes, I did take the train this morning. My point of departure was a small village in Scotland which lies between Carlisle and Edinburgh. I was drawn up there yesterday morning when I learned from the local constabulary that they might have a lead on my case. The matter, on the surface, is a simple one, Mr. Holmes, but I fear that I have been diverted by some of the more *fantastic* elements of the problem.

"What you must first understand about the locality, Mr. Holmes, is that this isolated hamlet is almost entirely cut off from civilization. The place, unlikely to be found on any map, is called Reavermere and is sparsely populated by only a few residents who live in homes scattered across what I assume constitutes the township. There is only one spot of any particular note and that is the ancestral home of the Broadbridge family which has lived in the region since the days of the feudal serfs. I shall return to the master of the estate,

Charles Broadbridge, later. The desolation which marks Reavermere makes it the ideal locality for clandestine meetings or matters of intrigue to take place should I believe that the populace was capable of such a thing. It is the outsiders who have brought the intrigue to Reavermere, and those outsiders have taken the form of a group of youths from both Scotland and England.

"It appears that a group of young men and women – some of them barely older than that pageboy who you employ from time to time, Mr. Holmes – have converged on Reavermere to protest the colonial conflict which is transpiring in northern Africa. You know how young people can be, Mr. Holmes: they are yearning to rebel and it seems that these young bloods in particular have chosen to rebel against the establishment in the most curious display that I have ever heard of. Over the course of three nights they had intended to burn three wooden men. The symbolism of such an exercise was lost on me completely, but the practice – so I am told – had some precedent."

"Indeed," Holmes interjected, "there is some historical documentation of the druids erecting large effigies of men made of wicker and burning them as parts of their rituals. There was even documentation that these rituals often involved animal or human sacrifice to the gods."

I barely contained an astonished "good lord" at the notion that something so archaic was being practiced in the nineteenth century.

"You were quite right," Holmes continued with a bemused grin, "you have brought me something *recherché*, inspector. You have, however, done a spectacular job at refusing to tell me what crime has been committed that brought you from Scotland to London."

"One of these youths," Gregson said, "has disappeared. The girl, Alice Bentley, disappeared from her home here in London three nights ago. Alice was the daughter of prominent barrister, Albert Bentley, who contacted the Yard when it was discovered that a number of his daughter's clothes were missing and the window to her room was found open. Naturally, Bentley suspected foul play and, fearing that his daughter had been abducted, my men and I launched an immediate investigation. I was fortunate enough to speak to a few of Alice Bentley's friends and they told me that they had heard whispers of Alice running off with a few of her other friends to Scotland and attending this burning man ceremony. I was able to get a list of the friends' name and cross-referenced them with the names of those passengers who had traveled by train to Scotland three days ago. There was a match and so I left for Reavermere first thing yesterday morning. I spent all of the day investigating and speaking to a number of the youths, but I learned nothing. If any of them knew Alice Bentley, they were being quite tight-lipped about it."

"What of the girl's friends?" I asked. "Were you able to locate them?"

"Yes," Gregson replied. "The three adolescents whom I was told were acquainted with Alice – Toby Smith, Douglas Williams, and Christine Martin – all said that Alice never came with them. They all seemed like legitimate responses from three surprisingly upstanding young persons. I know how children are though, Mr. Holmes; they will go to extreme lengths to protect their friends and I believe that that is precisely the case here."

"You spoke of a house owned by one Charles Broadbridge," Holmes said. "What role does he play in this narrative?"

"The estate of Broadbridge Manor extends nearly thirty acres in all directions from the house itself. It was on his grounds that the adolescents erected their wooden effigy. I spoke with him for some time yesterday, and he told me that he knew nothing of the business. Indeed, he hardly knew of the children's presence on his estate at all. He was only informed that morning by a gamekeeper that they had chosen his land to camp out."

"You also spoke of the local constabulary," Holmes continued.

"That is the queerest part of the whole business," Gregson said, getting drawn into his own story once more. "One girl – Anna Steinway – claims to have seen Alice Bentley the night of her disappearance. It was she who reported the disappearance in the first place and, fortuitously, I was wiring the constabulary about my case when they wired to the Yard in need of help."

"I should think," I interjected, "that the simplest explanation should be the correct one. Obviously, Alice Bentley did run away from home and travel to Scotland with a few of her friends. This girl, Anna Steinway, must have been mistaken – it seems certainly possible that she was caught up in the lunacy of such a situation – and reported

Alice as missing. When word got around that that had occurred, the local police began their own investigation. Alice knew that she would be found and asked for her friends to fabricate a story that she had never gone."

"I am inclined to agree with the doctor," Gregson said, "but all-the-same, you must admit that the case is a tantalizing one, Mr. Holmes."

"It is certainly singular if nothing else," Holmes replied. "I confess that you have piqued my curiosity, Gregson. I was bemoaning only this morning that nothing singular has come my way in some time and now you proven me quite, quite wrong. With nothing else on hand it would be remiss of me not to accompany you back to Scotland and see the lay of my land myself."

"Then you do believe that Alice Bentley is in Scotland and not still here in London?"

"I do not reject the possibility that she is, outright," Holmes countered. "I should still have one of your men – or another inspector, perhaps – look into things here. Though I believe that it would be fruitless for us to remain here in the city when the true intrigue of this case lies to the north, might I suggest that you mend some of the burned bridges you have created with your colleague, Mr. Lestrade, and have him handle the details of the case here in the city?"

I saw the faintest hint of a look of chagrin cross Gregson's face. I looked to Holmes and saw a ghost of a smile cross his. I knew that, inwardly, he derived some pleasure from the petty competition between Inspectors Gregson and Lestrade.

"In the meantime," Holmes said turning to me, "perhaps you would make a long arm, Watson, and find in *Bradshaw's* when the next train for Scotland leaves. If memory serves it will be the 12.09 to Edinburgh and from there I surmise that a cross-country carriage ride shall be in our future. We can only hope that the rain does not persist as it has or we shall be soaked to the bone before the investigation has even commenced."

Our journey by train was carried out in moderate silence. Gregson and I endeavored to peer out of the rain-streaked compartment windows while Holmes sat wrapped up in his own thoughts as he peered at a map of the region we were entering. My friend cut an impressive figure clad in his Inverness cape and ear-flapped travelling cap under the brim of which his grey eyes darted across the sheet of foolscap.

As Holmes had suggested, our train arrived in Edinburgh long after nightfall, and it appeared as if we had brought the rain from London with us. While my friend went about securing us a wagonette to travel the some considerable distance to the hamlet of Reavermere, Gregson sent off a wire to Charles Broadbridge. Though Holmes had shown little interest in speaking to the nobleman, the inspector explained that his hospitality would afford us a warm place to stay should the investigation prove more complex than we had figured. As

I stood on the station platform, my arms folded about my middle in a vain attempt to hug my greatcoat to my body for more warmth, I could not thank the Scotland Yarder enough for the prospect of a fire, a warm bed, and perhaps a drink to take the chill off of my bones.

Holmes returned a few moments later with a carriage and driver in toe. We clambered aboard and spent an interminable period of time rattling along a series of long, desolate roads which ran amongst the undulating hills of Scotland. Had I been in a cheerier disposition, I would have taken in the countryside with appreciation and found the green hills which stretched out before me to be a lovely indicator of the summer which had passed still clinging on as autumn took hold of the countryside. In time, this lush vista would be white with new-fallen snow and the trees which lined the road would be bare and free of the rich leaves which still hung on their branches. But, as we rode on through the downpour, I could think of nothing more than being out of the cold and rain.

The great house which loomed in the distance as we drew near was like a beacon of hope to us. Our irritable group was surely ready for the warmth and comfort as our carriage drew up by the great double doors which, in days gone by, must have stood out as an impressive display of wealth. Even today, I said to myself as I hopped down from my perch in the back of the carriage, the great mansion was a testament to the longevity of a prominent family, and the wealth which accompanied generations of living off of such opulent land.

We drew inside the great main hall of the house which had been done over in marble. A staircase ascended to the second story of the house and, within the foyer, the roof appeared to be supported by great columns which would not have looked out of place holding up the Parthenon. A servant relieved us of our sopping wet clothes and I was grateful to be led into a large, equally lavish library which was just off of the main hall. Standing before a large fireplace was the man I took to be Charles Broadbridge himself. An impressive man dressed in form-fitting tweeds, I took him to be no older than forty. Surely, I told myself, if he were, he was certainly one of the most spry-looking specimens upon whom I had ever clapped eyes.

"Inspector Gregson," he said warmly as the three of us drew into the library, a room lined with bookshelves seemingly floor-to-ceiling, "how good of you to return. Please, take a seat before the fire."

I traced no accent in his speech.

"It is you whom I should be thanking," Gregson said. "Your hospitality is far too generous." Broadbridge batted away the notion with a wave of the hand. "Allow me to introduce my colleagues," Gregson continued, "Mr. Sherlock Holmes and Dr. John Watson."

Holmes and I extended our hands. "It is a pleasure, Mr. Holmes," Broadbridge said. "I have heard your name on a number of occasions when I am down in London."

"You are far too kind, Mr. Broadbridge," the detective replied.

"I can only imagine what you make of this whole business," Broadbridge said to Holmes as he moved to the sideboard and proffered us all drinks which we readily accepted. "I will answer any and all questions which you may have to pose to me."

"Should I have the need, I will do so and your cooperation is appreciated," Holmes replied. "However, Mr. Broadbridge, I shouldn't think that you will be needed in the unraveling of this mystery. As I learned from Inspector Gregson, you were unaware of the adolescents' presence on your land until yesterday morning."

"That is correct," Broadbridge replied. "I sent my gamekeeper out yesterday and was quite surprised when he reported back that about fifteen young people were camped out there around a mound of ashes. I have since come to learn that they had built some wooden effigy in protestation against the Mahdist War. It sounded like quite an unusual bit of business, but it did not seem that they had done much harm. That was until I learned about the disappearing girl."

"And, according to Inspector Gregson," I said, "you knew nothing about her either."

"That is correct, Dr. Watson," Broadbridge replied. "In fact, I had never clapped eyes on any of the children until yesterday morning and none of them looked to me like Alice Bentley."

As if he knew what query we would next pose, Tobias Gregson reached into his inner pocket and withdrew a photograph of a young girl whom I took to be little more than sixteen years of age. She was a pretty young girl with a pleasant face and blonde curls.

"You are certain that no one – none of the adolescents – looked like her?" Holmes asked, posing his question to both Gregson and Broadbridge.

"No," the Inspector answered. "Alice Bentley's father supplied me with that photograph and the very first thing I did when I arrived here was to compare everyone to that picture. It yielded nothing."

"Though you hardly have the most perceptive eye," Holmes retorted, "I do not doubt you in this case, Gregson. At present, then, I'm afraid that we are still very much in the dark. We have little to go off, other than the insistence of the girl, Anna Steinway that Alice Bentley was here in Reavermere. It is she, then, that we should endeavor to speak to next. Did you question Anna Steinway, inspector?"

"Yes, but –"

Holmes held up a hand in protestation. "I am afraid that you have biased my view of this case enough, inspector. I think it best that we speak to her now. Where is she?"

"At the constable's office," Gregson replied. "It is only a short drive from here."

"Excellent," Holmes said jumping to his feet. "Then that shall be our next port of call. Thank you for your hospitality, Mr. Broadbridge. Perhaps we could impose upon you for dinner upon our return?"

"No imposition at all!"

"Good," said Holmes as he started for the door, "then it is time that we begin to get to the heart of this matter. Gentlemen, let us be off."

Sherlock Holmes was certainly not without a touch of the dramatic, especially during a case, yet it took Gregson and me a few seconds to process his most grandiose of exits. We hastened after him and found the detective in the foyer shrugging on his Inverness and taking up his deerstalker in his gloved hands. The inspector and I quickly bundled up our own greatcoats and followed Holmes out into the chilled evening air. The sun had by now disappeared over the horizon lending an ominous air to the rainy evening. The carriage which we had arrived in had parked itself before the front doors of the mansion and, climbing in once more, we started off down the long, desolate path away from Broadbridge Manor.

As we rode – the moon, passing in and out of the clouds – provided our only source of illumination. As the shadows crept long around us, I thought, at first, that my eyes were deceiving me when I spied movement not far off from the path. As if he could divine my thoughts, Inspector Gregson leaned over to me and spoke against the rain whipping around us.

"That is the campsite of the youths," he explained.

"You mean to say that they are still here on the property?"

"Broadbridge has filed no compliant against them," Gregson replied. "In fact, he seems to have taken something of a liking to their unique form of protest."

Sherlock Holmes interjected, seeming to have taken no notice of our conversation, "How far is it to the constable's office?"

"Only a mile or so down the road," Gregson replied. "It is one of the few buildings here in Reavermere."

Our carriage trundled past a dense thicket and, once we had skirted the forest, we emerged onto another plain sparsely populated by infrequent outcroppings of stone buildings. Our carriage drew up outside of one and we disembarked, finding ourselves in a low, but comfortable room outfitted with little more than few chairs, a desk, and a fireplace. There were two occupants in the room: a small, round man in his early forties who I took to the constable, and a young girl who could have been none other than Anna Steinway.

"Ah, welcome back," said the constable, rising from his seat and addressing Gregson. The two officers of the law shook hands.

"Mr. Holmes, Dr. Watson, allow me to introduce Sergeant Burke of the Reavermere Constabulary."

Holmes and I shook hands with Burke who returned to his seat and leaned back in his chair. His hairless, round face smiled pleasantly at the two of us as he gestured for us to sit.

"I must admit, gentlemen," Burke said in a thick, Scottish accent, "that is surely the strangest case that I have ever undertaken here in Reavermere."

"I should imagine that crime is quite uncommon in this region," I said.

"Quite right, sir. Quite right. My role is usually to settle disputes amongst the locals. Something of a professional mediator." Burke chuckled in spite of himself. "This is the first time that I have ever been put in a position such as this. From what I heard Inspector Gregson say about your methods, Mr. Holmes, it sounds as if I shall be in good hands, indeed." Again, the little man chuckled. Holmes's face betrayed little and if he found any amusement in the awkward position of the Reavermere police representative, he did not show it.

"Perhaps, then," Holmes said, "I may speak with Miss Steinway?"

The little girl who was seated on the other side of the room looked in our direction for the first time since we had entered the room. She was perhaps no older than fifteen and, despite a certain amount of nervousness which I detected in her eyes, she seemed to carry herself with a certain confidence seldom found in children her age. She was dressed in clothes which would have been more befitting of a man, I observed.

Burke gestured for Anna Steinway to join us. With some hesitation, she rose out of her seat and took the only unoccupied chair near Holmes, Gregson, and myself. In a soothing tone, Burke introduced both Holmes and me to the girl who nodded understandingly in our direction.

"I understand, Anna," Holmes said, affecting the most sensitive of tones, "that you have already spoken to Inspector Gregson about Alice – the girl who has disappeared. If you could repeat what you told him and answer any questions which I may pose to you, it would be much appreciated."

Anna Steinway drew in a deep breath, steadying herself in doing so. "I suppose the only place to begin is in London. I'm from London and, a week ago, I learned from a few of my friends that a group of girls were planning on something big. They were going to sneak away from home and join a group of others who were going to take the train to Scotland. I didn't know why they were going to do it, but it sounded terribly exciting. My friends and I planned on joining in. We didn't really know any of the children who had organized the whole thing, but we hoped that maybe, once we got to the station they wouldn't very well turn us away. Well, I snuck out and managed to get to the station only to find that none of my friends was there. I guess they either turned coward at the last minute or were caught by their parents."

"Do your parents know where you are now, Alice?" Holmes asked.

"Her parents have been contacted," Burke cut in. Holmes thanked the sergeant with a nod and gestured for the girl to continue.

"I didn't want to admit defeat, sir, so I jumped aboard the train anyway. It was now a matter of finding someone to travel with. I figured that if I went alone, I would have a hard time of things. By good fortune, I was able to share a compartment with Alice Bentley. I'd never met Alice before, but we got on quite well. She was only a year older than me, but she seemed so much more confident than I.

We both shared a laugh when the conductor came to collect our tickets and saw us without a chaperone. He said that he would have a word with someone about us – and no doubt the compartments filled with the other children – but Alice sent him away as though she were a real noblewoman speaking to a servant. It was delicious, sir!

"When we arrived in Scotland, Alice introduced me to her other friends: Toby, Douglas, and Christine. It transpired that it was Christine who had arranged the whole protest and we began our long trek to our campsite."

"You traveled by foot?" I asked.

Anna Steinway nodded. "It was a long walk, but Christine assured us that our long walk would only foster in us a greater belief in our cause and make us even more grateful for the plot of land we were staying on."

"Did Christine mention ever having been on the estate before?"

"No," Anna Steinway replied, "but she said that she was a frequent visitor to Scotland. Apparently, her family did some business in Edinburgh quite often and they traveled by carriage through Reavermere on occasion.

"When we finally arrived, I was exhausted as were the other fourteen of us. We threw ourselves down on the soft grass and just slept. When we awoke, the sun had gone down and Christine was preparing for the ritual burning of the wooden man."

A faint chill based down the base of my spine at these most unusual words.

"While I had slept," Anna continued, "a few of the other children had gone off into the woods and gathered some wood and put together a *man*. In fact, they had found so many that there were plans to build two more identical ones. Torches were lit and, from her bag, Christine produced a bottle of something which she passed around to all of us. I cannot say what it was exactly, but it was certainly strong and, taking a big swig of it made me feel dizzy and pretty sick to my stomach. But, it put us all in a celebratory mood as we set fire to the large man. Not long after though, things became a bit hazy and we all awoke on the grass once more."

"During this celebration," Holmes said, "did you see Alice Bentley?"

"She and I were together almost all the time," Anna Steinway replied. "It was only when I awoke that I found she was no longer about. I searched our little campsite and even searched the woods. I dared not go too far into them for fear that I might get lost. I roused a few of the other children and either they did not know Alice at all or they had not seen her since the ceremony the previous evening. I had remembered Christine pointing out to us the police station on our walk into town the previous day and I made my way there at once."

"Anna," Sherlock Holmes said, his soothing voice continuing to put the child at ease, "why should Alice's friends – Christine, Toby, and Douglas – say that Alice never came with them on this trip?"

"You cannot begin to imagine, sir," Anna Steinway replied, quite candidly, "what would happen if we were found out. It would be trouble enough explaining our disappearance if we lied and said that we stayed in London. To say that we ventured to Scotland is another prospect entirely."

Holmes smiled the ghost of a grin and tapped his long index finger to his lips. "Thank you, Anna," he said at length, "you have been of considerable assistance to me. And, I must applaud you for your forthrightness and willingness to answer my questions. You are quite an impressive young woman."

Anna Steinway smiled in response to my friend's warm words.

From his waistcoat pocket, Holmes withdrew his watch. "It is getting late," he said, "and I fear that little more shall be accomplished this night. Perhaps we ought to return to Broadbridge Manor and take Mr. Broadbridge up on his offer of a late supper. And then, to bed. I suspect another long day ahead of us, gentlemen. I should very much like to speak with Christine Martin, for I am beginning to suspect that she may hold many of the answers to this most unusual of problems. And, what is more, I should very much like to meet another character in this drama; one about whom we have heard a great deal."

"And who might that be, Mr. Holmes?" Gregson asked.

Sherlock Holmes smiled. "Why, the burning man, of course."

The rain had let up the following morning which left a low-hanging fog curling about the ground. As I woke and peered out my window, I lost the lush green grass beneath the impenetrable, swirling mist, and I was put in mind of a foggy evening in London. I washed and dressed and descended the stairs to the main dining room to find that I had risen before either Holmes or our guest. I had found myself incredibly fatigued after the strenuous day and after the post-dinner drinks had excused myself early to bed. Holmes had not taken part in the libations, excusing himself after barely touching his meal. He had been customarily quiet during dinner, leaving me to engage Charles Broadbridge in polite conversation. When I had retired to bed, I had last seen Holmes seated in a chair in the library engrossed in a large, weathered-looking tome.

My fast was broken with the help of a servant who served a plate of eggs and toast and in short order, Broadbridge, Gregson, and Holmes joined me in the dining room. I noticed dark circles under my friend's eyes, speaking to a sleepless night. I said as much as Holmes accepted a cup of coffee.

"I was running through a number of the facts which we gained yesterday evening in my mind," Holmes replied as he took a sip of coffee. "You need not stare me down like that, Watson," he added as a good-natured barb. "I can sleep aplenty when this case is through and, besides," he gestured to his cup, "this makes for a fine stimulant to rouse me from my early-morning fatigue."

I brushed aside Holmes's remarks with a chuckle.

"You still intend to speak to Christine Martin this morning?" Gregson asked.

"Very much so," Holmes retorted. "As she was the organizer of this most unique of events, I feel as though she can shed much light on this case. And, of course, I must still get a glimpse of the fabled wooden man."

"Would you care for me to accompany you this morning, gentlemen?" Broadbridge asked.

"I would not think to trouble you," Holmes replied. "I think between the three of us, Dr. Watson, the inspector, and I can find our way about the grounds. But, come, gentlemen. We waste our time shut up in doors when the answers to this mystery lie outside."

Holmes excused himself from the table and Gregson and I rushed after him. Once we had outfitted ourselves in our greatcoats and hats, we began the walk down the path towards the edge of the Broadbridge estate. Our walk through the sodden ground felt like an interminable one, but at length we came upon the small encampment of youths; each of them staring at us as though we were a different breed entirely. I had felt the same, confused stare many times in my life. Though Holmes had made employ of a number of street urchins in London – and each of them respected him as though he were their father – I had never been quite able to connect with them. There was a certain amount of begrudging respect, I think, that the children paid me, but to them, I fear that I was little more than another *toff*.

Disposing with decorum immediately, Holmes called out to the group to speak to Christine Martin. At first, we received no answer. However, a moment later, from amongst the crowd of youths, a tall, young woman stood and advanced towards us. She was dressed in a simple, flowing dress; the kind which would have looked very becoming on a debutante, appearing for her first season in society. There was something dark and mysterious about the girl, I noticed. Her eyes flashed and her dark hair hung down about her shoulders. I noticed too that Christine Martin was barefoot. She was, I surmised, the kind of free spirit which even the most stringent of societal rules could not tame.

"Gentlemen," Christine Martin said, as she drew up before us. "How may I be of service to you?"

"Miss Martin," Holmes said, adopting the same calming tone which he had employed on the young Anna Steinway the night before, "my name is Sherlock Holmes. I have been consulted by Scotland Yard to look into the disappearance of Alice Bentley from your group. We know as well as you that she was amongst your party so you can dispense with your cover-up. I believe that you may be able to supply us with some very necessary answers and would be most grateful for your assistance, Miss Martin."

Christine Martin's dark eyes were unreadable. Though she held herself with the poise of a woman beyond her years, I had to remind myself that she was, indeed, only a young girl. What she must have been thinking, though, I simply could not divine.

At length she responded, "If there is anything that I can do to help, I shall be happy to do so."

"As I understand it from Inspector Gregson," Holmes began, "you are the organizer of this protest."

"What exactly were you trying to accomplish?" I interjected without thinking.

"We were trying to be noticed," Christine Martin retorted.

"By whom?" Gregson said coldly.

"Someone," she retorted. "We have long enough been ignored by our own kith and kin. It is high time that someone notices what we stand for. Taking notice of us is the only way that we will stop sending thousands of innocent men to die for fruitless causes. I have lived all my life, gentlemen, in the upper echelons of society and it is deemed an honor to die for your country. But, I have seen what it does. What it does to families. To friends. This bloodshed must end somehow, and we want to be noticed. The great might of the Roman Empire stopped and took notice when the Druids created wooden effigies of men and burned them. We hope that the great might of our government might stop and take notice of us too."

I admit I was impressed by the young woman's rhetoric, but all I could manage was a grumbled, "I rather think you have succeeded in being noticed."

Holmes silenced me with a glare. "You were close friends with Alice Bentley," Holmes said, seeming to have ignored

Christine's impassioned speech. "Over the course of the past few days, how often have you seen her?"

"We saw each other off at the train station in London," Christine replied. "We were separated from there as I shared a compartment with Douglas and Toby. When we all arrived here in Reavermere, I caught sight of her again and she seemed to be in good spirits. She was spending a great deal of her time with Anna Steinway; a girl I had never met, but I applauded her efforts in joining our little group nevertheless."

"And after the night of your arrival," Holmes continued, "you did not see her after that? I am informed by Miss Steinway that you all consumed a large portion of *something* which put you all to sleep."

Christine Martin smiled. "A sampling of the local aqua vitae," she replied. "I confess that none of us truly had the stomach for the stuff."

"But you too saw nothing then during the night, and when you came to Alice Bentley was gone?"

"That is correct, Mr. Holmes."

"What I don't understand," said Tobias Gregson who had stood by in silence up until this moment, "is why you all refused to acknowledge that Alice Bentley was a member of this group when first questioned."

"You cannot begin to fathom, sir, the amount of trouble which we will all be in when word reaches our parents' ears what we are doing. Should Alice Bentley have been discovered amongst us, the consequences of fleeing to the north will be harsh ones indeed."

"I have heard much talk of the wooden man," Holmes said, "and I understand that a few of them were erected. Would it be possible to see one up close?"

My eye was drawn to the mound of ash which stood only feet from where we now were. The remaining children sat around it, talking in hushed tones. There was something unnerving about the ash, I considered; its inky darkness offset by the lushness of the greenery which surrounded us. My mind still boggled at the queerness of the whole situation and how it could transpire here in the nineteenth century. As if he could read my thoughts, Sherlock Holmes said:

"There are more things in heaven and earth, Watson, than are dreamt of in your philosophy."

I turned to face my friend and saw that he and Gregson were slowly moving away from where I stood, following two young men towards the thicket. I caught up to them and our small group made our way into the outcropping of trees and brush. As we made our way over branches and fallen leaves which crunched underfoot, I had a sudden impression that the further we moved into this forest, the more we were moving away from modernity. Already, I reasoned, we found ourselves staying on an estate which had existed since the time of the serfs in an isolated part of the country cut off from the outside world. I suddenly felt very insignificant in the vastness of our surroundings and, so caught up in my thoughts was I that I very nearly ran into

Gregson's back when we all stopped and stared at the strange figure which stood before us.

A wooden man it was, or at least it appeared to have assumed the shape of a man. I detected the outline of a round head and arms at its side, outstretched, and resembling – albeit in the crudest form – the Vitruvian Man. This figure was born from masses of branches and twigs which had been bound together by rope; each limb, in turn, tied together to form this figure which now towered over us. I judged that the wooden man must have been about ten feet in height and nearly six feet wide. Surely, I figured, it was no simple task to assemble such a curious monolith.

Holmes stepped forward and examined the figure. I heard him murmur inaudibly under his breath and so caught up in his investigation was I that I was once more taken by surprise when I heard the voice of Christine Martin from behind me:

"Impressive is it not, Mr. Holmes?"

"I must admit that I have never seen anything quite like it in my life," Holmes replied. "I must ask; how was it made?"

Christine gestured to the young man who had been our guide.

"It was assembled," he said in the most methodical tone, "by first assembling the arms and legs of the man. We gathered together as many bundles of sticks as we could and, in certain cases, we wrenched branches off trees if we figured they could make for better support. The torso and head were saved for last and the head was affixed to the rest of the body from inside. As you can see, the man is hollow."

"I applaud the effort which obviously went into creating it," Holmes said. "I must imagine that you and your party attracted some attention in setting the man up where you did?"

"Hardly, Mr. Holmes," Christine replied. "Reavermere is, as you will have noticed, quite isolated. In all of our time in setting up the burning man, only one carriage drove past. It, I recognized, as belonging to Mr. Broadbridge himself. He seemed to have been returning from some outing or another with another gentleman."

Sherlock Holmes smiled the ghost of a grin. "Miss Martin," he said, "you have been most kind in answering all of my questions and for allowing us to catch a glimpse of the fabled burning man. And, if I may go so far as to say, you are the very model of an English gentlewoman. Your forthrightness and independence are admirable qualities indeed."

I thought I heard Miss Martin scoff under her breath, but she nevertheless thanked my friend and our party advanced out of the forest and into the clearing once more. After we had excused ourselves from the group of youths, Gregson turned to Holmes, a look of stupefaction etched on his countenance.

"Well, Mr. Holmes," he said, "I cannot for the life of me imagine that you gained anything special from all that questioning. You have learned nothing that we didn't already know last night."

"On the contrary, inspector," Holmes smugly replied. "I confess to you both that I have, for some hours now, been holding more cards in my hands then it seems I was originally dealt. The pieces of this puzzle are beginning to fall into place but, they are at present, founded entirely upon conjecture and I am, therefore, hesitant to reveal them to you now."

"Oh, dash it all, Holmes," I said. "I think that we have all been through quite enough in the past few days. I believe that you owe us an explanation or two."

"Your persistence is admirable in the extreme, Watson," Holmes said, as he clapped me on the shoulder. "Very well. I shall draw your attention to a few items of information which I believe ought to set your minds working in the right direction towards solving this mystery. But, let us set our sights back towards the Broadbridge house for our answers do lie there."

Holmes started off on foot once more leaving Gregson and me to bustle after him.

"You will doubtlessly recall," Holmes began, "that when I pressed Inspector Gregson in our rooms at Baker Street for the role Mr. Broadbridge played in this story, the inspector confessed that it was a decidedly minimal one. In fact, the inspector said, when questioned, Charles Broadbridge had no knowledge of the youths' presence on his land until he was informed of the fact by his gamekeeper. This fact was refuted only moments ago when Christine

Martin said that she saw Broadbridge ride by in his carriage as they set up the first wooden man three days ago.

"Put yourself in the position of a wealthy landowner: you see a number of undesirable-looking characters camped out on your estate. Surely your first instinct is to send them away. But, it sounds as though Broadbridge did not do this. Charles Broadbridge knew that they were on his land much earlier than he said that he did. So, I must ask myself, why did he lie?

"The next piece of the puzzle fell into place last evening. I observed you stick your head into the library, Watson, after dinner and saw me engrossed in a book. It was a well-worn old volume; a history of the British Isles. It is, of course, the sort of history which could put anyone suffering from insomnia to sleep, but I did find in it one point of interest. It was clear to me that the book had been recently opened. It sat on a shelf next to myriad other volumes which had each been arranged neatly, and yet it had been placed back with its brethren in the most haphazard of manners. Someone had consulted that volume with extreme haste and returned it quickly to the shelf hoping that no one would be any the wiser."

"But what could have been so important?"

"Have you not already guessed? From the outset of this investigation, ancient history has had a hand in this odd business. When Inspector Gregson informed us of the wooden men, I instantly recalled reading of the druidic ceremonies and, just today, Christine Martin referenced the same ancient people. Though, to many, the burning man ceremonies have become a lost chapter in English history, I found a complete write-up of the ceremonies in that old tome last evening. When you put these two pieces of information together, you can only come to one inevitable conclusion:

"Charles Broadbridge has been lying to us from the outset."

"But, what would be his motive for doing so?" Gregson asked. "Broadbridge has no connection whatsoever with the disappearing girl."

"You are too myopic, inspector," Holmes retorted. "This case does not hinge upon the disappearance of Alice Bentley. In fact, her vanishing is merely the result of a far darker scheme. Remember what Christine Martin said: she observed Broadbridge riding in his carriage with another man. What has become of this second individual? We have seen neither hide nor hair of any other guest while we have been staying at the manor house."

"Are you insinuating...*murder*?" I asked.

"If it has not already been committed, then attempted murder at the very least," Holmes replied. "Think of it! You lure a man to your home to do away with him. At present, the man's identity and the motive for wishing him dead, I do not know. But, with him in your grasp, you concoct a scheme to kill him and surely dispose of his body in the woodland. Reavermere is an isolated hamlet with a police force which is not accustomed to solving true crimes. But, there is always the chance that something could go amiss. What if this man has relatives or friends who begin to look into his disappearance, much in the way that you, Gregson, were called in to investigate the missing Alice Bentley? You cannot risk the discovery of a corpse. And then, as if by providence, you see a group of people camping out on your estate and erecting what looks like a large, wooden man. You are naturally confused. But then you recall that portion of the history book in your library. You consult it once more and learn that the wooden man will be burned as part of a ceremony and *voila*, the perfect means by which you can dispose of a body have been dropped into your lap.

"I admit, gentlemen, that the case is based on theories alone, at present, but I defy you to come up with another explanation which fits with the facts as we know them."

"But the business with the missing girl," Gregson said, "how the devil does she fit into all of this?"

"As I said, inspector, Alice Bentley's disappearance comes as a result of Charles Broadbridge's murder scheme. Perhaps, in an effort to divert attention away from himself, Broadbridge takes his victim outdoors and onto the grounds of the estate to do away with him. He murders him and is in the process of hiding his body when he realizes that he has been observed. Perhaps Alice Bentley was able to stomach the concoction which Christine Martin proffered to the assembled group better than anyone else and awoke from her drunken slumber early; early enough to witness the culmination of a diabolical scheme come to fruition. Broadbridge has now been seen and he must do something."

"Good lord, Holmes," I said, "you don't mean to say that he has…killed the poor girl."

"I pray that he has not," Holmes replied darkly. "Broadbridge is a desperate man, but I hazard a guess that even he could not stoop so low. However, we tread in territory which I do not like and I cannot speak to what has or has not happened to poor Alice Bentley."

"Well, if Broadbridge has killed a man," Gregson said, "and hasn't disposed of his body yet, then where do you suppose he has hidden it?"

Holmes stopped and considered. "I should imagine that the place we would want to begin searching is in the gamekeeper's cottage. I cannot think of a better man to take into your confidence than another who lives on the estate in an out-of-the-way abode. However, I do not know if the man is in at present and, seeing as we are all unarmed, forcing our way in could mean certain death to us all."

"For once I can correct you, Holmes," I said. "I have taken to seldom leaving Baker Street without my service revolver. It's in my trunk now."

"Good man!" Holmes beamed. "Then let us return to the Broadbridge house and I shall put a question to Mr. Broadbridge concerning his gamekeeper. If it sounds as though the cottage will be empty then Watson and I shall investigate further. I must insist, Gregson that you stay behind and keep an eye on Mr. Broadbridge. He is a desperate man who is playing a bold game, and in my experience, those people are the ones you must be most fearful of."

We made little show of our return to the manor house. I stole up to my room and plucked my revolver from between the shirts and trousers which I had packed, and slipped it into the inner pocket of greatcoat. Returning downstairs, I found the Inspector, Holmes, and Broadbridge standing before a very welcoming-looking fire in the library.

"Good news, Watson," Holmes said, feigning a bemused tone as I entered, "Mr. Broadbridge says that his gamekeeper has gone into town and will not be back until late afternoon. I told him that we wished to walk about the estate but we did not want to catch him off-guard."

"You hear stories, you know," Broadbridge said, "of trigger-happy gamekeepers. Sad, truly." Though he spoke with no malice, I felt as if Charles Broadbridge's words were boring into my very soul. I feared that he might be onto us at any moment.

"I suggest that we set off at once then," Holmes said crossing to me and taking me by the elbow. "I fear that rain is in the foreseeable future and I think we were soaked trough enough last evening. Are you coming, inspector?"

"No," Gregson replied as he took a seat on the sofa. "I think that I shall stay here and rest my feet. I am not as nimble as you, Mr. Holmes."

Holmes and I chuckled and then we set off out of the house and started to make our way across the vast lawn.

As we turned our backs on the mansion, I suddenly was filled with the strangest feeling as though the house were watching us retreat across the estate. Its broad windows and turrets seemed to be staring us down and I felt irrelevant under its domineering stare. Holmes, however, seemed to be as determined as ever. In case, he informed me, we were being observed from the house, we made a direct route for the woodland and, once under the cover of the thicket, we made our way towards the cottage which Holmes informed me he had taken to finding the previous evening. It was a small, stone building covered in ivy and set back in a grove of trees which we came upon at the end of our journey. As we approached, I realized that were quite vulnerable as we approached and I sincerely hoped that Broadbridge suspected nothing and that the gamekeeper was, indeed, not at home.

Holmes went to the front door first and rapped upon it. Receiving no answer, he tried the knob and found that it too would not budge. Holmes wordlessly gestured for me to hand him my revolver. I reached into my coat and pressed the cold, dead steel into my friend's palm. Then, without a word, Holmes stepped back, planted his heel on the door and gave the whole thing a sound kick. The door splintered at the hinges and fell from the frame with a thud. Sweeping the gun from side to side as we entered, we stepped across the threshold and into the house proper.

The cottage was a small, but welcoming space. The room into which we entered was sparsely decorated save for a few chairs and a worn-looking settee. Over an empty hearth sat a gun rack and I realized, with a chill of anxiety that the shotgun which surely must be mounted there was missing.

"Holmes," I began, but was cut off by a friend's curt nod.

"Yes," he said, "I noticed too. Our friend the gamekeeper must not be far afield for a shotgun is hardly the proper item to take on a trip into town. Come, we had best find evidence of the murder or the missing Alice Bentley with haste."

We broke off into two directions as we scoured for any trace of any misdeed. I yielded nothing in a cursory search and, as I re-entered the sitting room, I found Holmes upon all fours on the ground.

"Blood," he observed, "trace drops of it are discernable on the floor. The floor has also been recently washed. It is evidently cleaner here than it is under the chair or the settee. You can observe for yourself, Watson. This is our greatest indicator of foul play thus far."

My friend stood, brushing himself off. I was about to speak, when he silenced me. It was only then that I heard a muffled sound coming from somewhere within the cottage. Holmes and I looked at each other knowingly: it must be Alice Bentley. With renewed vigor we searched the cottage again; this time, opening and closing doors in a whirlwind. At length, I came upon a cupboard door and, flinging it open, I found myself staring into the terrified eyes of a young girl. I recognized her instantly. I called out to Holmes and together we helped the terrified Alice Bentley to her feet. She had been bound with a length of twine about the wrists and ankles and, cutting through them, Alice burst into tears.

"It's alright," I said reassuringly, embracing the frightened child. "You're safe now. You're quite safe now."

"Miss Bentley," Holmes said, "I apologize for posing a question like this to you now, but can you say anything about the men who have kept you here?"

Alice Bentley tried to speak, but only a hoarse gasp escaped her lips.

"Tell me," Holmes added in his reassuring tone, "was one of the men a tall, broad-shouldered man most probably dressed in an expensive-looking suit?"

Alice Bentley nodded. Holmes let out a satisfied breath.

"Hardly the perfect testimony, Watson," Holmes said, "but Miss Bentley has surely just identified Charles Broadbridge. And, I am sure that once she has recovered from this ordeal, she will be quite capable of delivering a full report to Inspector Gregson. Come, let us get her back. I am sure the girl could use something to eat and drink."

As we prepared to lead Alice Bentley out of the cottage, we spotted a figure approaching the building and we three stopped dead in our tracks. I heard Holmes mutter an oath under his breath as he caught sight of the man who most surely was the gamekeeper approaching.

A moment later, the window nearest our heads exploded into a thousand shards of glass. Peering through the shattered pane, I perceived the gamekeeper taking aim with his shotgun and preparing to fire at us once more. So taken aback was I by the blast that I did not give my service revolver a second thought, and I jumped after Holmes and Alice. Crouched on the floor, I felt like a sitting duck, certain that my life was about to come to a very abrupt end.

However, much to my surprise, the next round was never fired. After what we judged to have an exceedingly long period of time, Holmes and I slowly got to our feet and stared out of the window. The gamekeeper was lying sprawled out on the ground and standing over him was a crowd of four youths; amongst them Christine Martin.

"It looks as if we owe these young people our lives," Holmes said to me.

We stepped outside with Alice Bentley and she ran into the arms of Christine Martin.

"We cannot thank you enough, Miss Martin," Sherlock Holmes said.

"You do not need to thank me," she replied. "However, you can retract your comment about my ladylike nature, Mr. Holmes. I daresay no *gentlewoman* in London would so willingly rush towards the sound of gunfire and wrestle a man to the ground."

Holmes and I both laughed. "I believe you are quite right in that assessment, Miss Martin," Holmes said. "Quite right."

The next few hours passed by in a blur. Returning to Gregson in the house, we managed to elicit a confession from Charles Broadbridge. It transpired that the dead man was one of Broadbridge's business partners, a man who had discovered some discrepancies in a number of financial ledgers. Despite, Broadbridge said, the history of money which existed in his family, he had lost a large portion of it to a series of bad investments and had begun embezzling in order to keep himself afloat. When his partner turned to threatening blackmail, Broadbridge concocted a scheme to murder him.

Gregson promised to keep us abreast of developments and assured us that Sergeant Burke of the Reavermere Constabulary would oversee the children. Holmes told the inspector that, if possible, he ought to convince the children's parents not to be too severe in the punishment of their sons and daughters. With our business all but concluded, Holmes and I soon found ourselves ensconced in a train compartment headed once more for London. Despite the successful conclusion to the entire business, Holmes seemed to lapse into a melancholic study once more as he peered out of the compartment windows at the undulating countryside which was slowly swallowed up by the night.

It was nearly midnight and, both of us still awake; I found it surprising when Holmes said:

"No one will believe you, I'm afraid."

"I beg your pardon?"

"This particular case," Holmes said, "from the start I described it as unique. Should it ever be made public, I believe that the masses would put it down as a farce. I know that you have drawn up records of our cases together, Watson, and I'm sure that you intend on doing much the same with this one as well. But, I warn you, it might be better for all concerned if the details of the mysterious case of the burning man go unspoken."

I considered for some time. "If that is what you wish, Holmes, then I shall abide by that."

A ghost of a smile crept across Holmes's stern mouth. "You know," he added, "you never did tell me what you think; the Mahdist War, I mean."

In all of the tumult of the past days, I had nearly forgotten how the whole strange business had begun. I bit my lip wondering just how to broach the topic with my friend. He had, after all, seemed quite taken with the speech delivered by Christine Martin. How, I wondered, could I attempt to speak to the contrary?

"Perhaps," I said at length, "the details of *that* should go unspoken too."

Holmes nodded knowingly. "Very well, doctor," he said leaning back in his chair, "we shall speak of it no more."

And, true to our word, we never did.

The Problem of the

Slashed Portrait

"Perhaps a doctor's opinion would be a viewpoint worth taking into account."

I stirred from the brown study into which I had fallen as I gazed out the rain-streaked bow window into the street which was conspicuously free of both foot traffic and carriages; most of London seeming to have taken refuge indoors and out of the tumult outside. Sherlock Holmes's voice had broken the silence which had fallen over the both of us for the better part of an hour, and I turned to him where he sat at his chemical workbench, the latest post near at hand.

"I would, of course, be happy to assist you with anything which may be on your mind," I said.

Holmes tossed across an opened envelope. "That letter has come from Mr. Thomas Fraser," he said, "the junior partner in the firm of Moorland and Fraser. The name will doubtlessly strike your ear as a familiar one?"

I nodded in the affirmative.

"He writes to me fearing for the sanity of his wife, Lucy Fraser."

Holmes stood from his seat and moved to his usual chair before the fire, reaching for his pipe and proceeding to fill it with tobacco from the toe of the Persian slipper which sat perched on the end of the mantelpiece.

"What has she done that prompts concern from Mr. Fraser," I asked.

Holmes struck a match and settled into his armchair. "Mrs. Fraser has taken a knife to a recently completed portrait of herself."

I arched an eyebrow in some surprise as Holmes blew a ring of bluish smoke about his head.

"Mr. Fraser writes about the whole ordeal in his letter," he said, "but let me save you the trouble of reading his correspondence for the time being. I'll go through the thing myself; see what details I can recall from memory before he arrives here to keep us up-to-date. Now then, I suppose I ought to begin with the Frasers. From what I understand – my finger is hardly on the pulse of such matters – the couple is the envy of high society. They are both in their early thirties and are happily married. Blight came to their marriage only very recently when Lucy was diagnosed with an anemic wasting disease which has confined her to her bed for some months.

"As to the portrait, it was being painted by Mr. Neville Devlin whose reputation precedes him in certain circles. He's a well-regarded artist, of the variety who caters to the elite, though somewhat derided for his Bohemian eccentricities – eccentricities which are no doubt no more unconventional than the majority of artists working in London, but warranting raised eyebrows and flared nostrils from the ruling class nevertheless. Devlin's studio is situated on the top floor of a building on The Strand and, despite her weakness, Mrs. Fraser always insisted on traveling there for her sittings while he painted her portrait.

"The incident which incited Fraser's writing to me occurred yesterday morning. For some weeks, Lucy Fraser's condition has been deteriorating and she has grown feebler by the day. Fraser was ready to call off the sitting with Devlin, but his wife insisted that she go: the portrait was very nearly done and sitting for it was always a highlight for her, she said. Fraser acquiesced to his wife's decision and they traveled across town, Lucy Fraser showing strength which she had not exhibited in some time as she climbed the steps to Devlin's studio. Fraser sat with her as he put the finishing touches on the portrait, serving them biscuits and tea as they finished. After nearly an hour of this, the artist set aside his brush and turned the canvas to face the lady. She looked at it for no more than a minute before she let out a shriek of rage, grabbed at a knife which sat on the breakfast table, and plunged it repeatedly into the canvas until the face of the painting was all but unrecognizable.

"That brings us to today, my dear fellow," Sherlock Holmes concluded. "Naturally, this display has made Fraser now not only fear for his wife's physical constitution, but her mental capacity as well. He said in his letter he had no one else to turn to, and decided to lay the matter before me, as my own reputation for clearing up little problems precedes me."

Holmes flashed a wry smile and languidly inspected his fingernails as he spoke. "What do you make of it all, Watson?"

I let out a sigh. "I can only suspect that Mrs. Fraser was overcome with emotion at finally seeing the completed portrait – a representation of the strong, healthy woman she once was before illness ravaged her so. Surely it was too much for her and she acted rashly in the moment."

"That is, of course, the simplest solution – and very often the stranger a thing seems the simpler its outcome is, but I feel trepidation in answering everything so easily. And I daresay that a man like Thomas Fraser would not bring the business to me should he have been able to clear it up as easily as that."

A moment later, the bell rang below and in short order Thomas Fraser was ushered into our sitting room. The young solicitor was a tall, broad-shouldered specimen with a handsome face and head of fair hair. He was well-dressed, his expensive coat bedewed with rain. I could at once see how this man would prompt the jealousy of so many, blessed as he was with both an enviable physical prowess and sizable purse as well. He shook hands with both Holmes and I and took a seat on the settee. He refused our offer of both drinks and cigars before Holmes returned to his chair and leaned forward to address our client directly:

"How fares your wife today, Mr. Fraser?"

"I have hardly been able to speak to Lucy at all this morning," he answered. "She's locked herself in her room and refuses to come out, instead sitting cooped up with weeks' worth of newspapers, poring over them as if they contained some secret to curing her. I have spoken to our housekeeper who says that Lucy has taken the key to her room with her, preventing anyone from entering the room. I endeavored to contact her doctor but she refuses to see him as well."

"You believe all of this was prompted by yesterday's episode with the portrait?"

"I know not what to think anymore, Mr. Holmes. I fear completely for Lucy's sanity. I know she has been ill for some time, and now I fear that her mind is going as well."

"Is there a history of mental instability in your wife's family?" I asked bluntly.

Fraser drew in a deep breath through his teeth. "Lucy's mother was never officially diagnosed, however Lucy has told me on more than one occasion that in her last days, her mother lost all her reason. She too locked herself in her room and refused any contact with the outside world. Within a week, the poor woman was dead."

Thomas Fraser blanched and I stood and poured him a drink from the sideboard which I pressed into his hand. He drank it begrudgingly. "I do not normally drink, doctor, but I thank you nevertheless."

"I am curious to know more about Mr. Neville Devlin," Holmes said at length. "I like to think of myself as an appreciator of art and yet I have never laid eyes on one of his works. From everything I understand, however, his is some of the finest in London."

"I consider myself very fortunate to know a genius like Devlin," Fraser replied. "He sees the world in a unique way which only an artist can truly grasp. When I thought of commissioning a portrait of Lucy he was the only man to whom I would entrust the job."

"How did you two meet?"

"He was in attendance at a party thrown by another friend of mine, Mrs. Cornelia Willis. Mrs. Willis likes to travel in the same Bohemian circles at which Devlin is the center. I took to him straight away…as did Lucy. Our kinship with him made it obvious that he was the man to paint her."

"And his other works solidified that in your mind?"

"Indeed. Devlin's studio is filled with numerous other portraits he's done in the past – each one so beautifully capturing the subject. I always thought that the completed painting would surely lift my dear Lucy's spirits."

A pregnant pause fell over the room, broken only by the tattoo of Holmes drumming his long fingers on the edge of the table at his side. At length, he eased back in his seat and exhaled deeply. "I always try to be frank with my clients, Mr. Fraser, and speaking thusly, I do not know what I can do for you. I have brought the matter to Dr. Watson's attention for I feel that this is a matter for a physician and not a detective. Your wife's case is a pretty little problem, indeed, but I do not wish to instill false hope."

Thomas Fraser's face fell. "There is nothing that you can do, Mr. Holmes?"

Sherlock Holmes held his index finger aloft. "Ah, that I did not say, Mr. Fraser. It would be remiss of me to cast you out seeing how dejected and crestfallen you are. I am, after all, in the business of solving problems, and you have presented me with a problem. I shall see what I can do, but working miracles is – I am afraid – even a little outside my own purview."

Fraser left our rooms perhaps not instilled with the confidence he would have hoped, but with some of the burden lifted from his shoulders. Once he had gone, Holmes turned to me, a look of concern etched deep on his pallid countenance.

"What's the matter?" I asked.

"I fear that we are treading in dark waters, Watson," Holmes replied, his voice hushed in a way which put me off considerably. "The business of Mrs. Lucy Fraser is quite outside the purviews of this agency's normal business, but if my intimation is accurate – which it often is – then we stray into territory to which we are more closely suited. And that is what concerns me so."

"You speak in riddles, Holmes."

Holmes paused again. "Put my ruminations out of your mind for the time being, Watson." A sudden alertness came into him and he dashed across the room to his index and began to flip through pages of press clippings hurriedly with the zeal of a hunter who has caught wind of his prey. "I confessed that I was not as familiar with the circles in which the Frasers traveled as I ought to be and I shall endeavor to rectify that presently. I fear that you shall find me inhospitable company for the time being, Watson."

I knew full well what this meant, but with little hope of venturing into the storm outside, I resigned myself to sitting in silence, coping with Holmes working his way through his strong shag tobacco pipe-full after pipe-full. It was gone three o'clock by the time that I heard him at last utter something under his breath – for so great was his concentration that he hardly spoke a word in the hours which elapsed since he began his study – and then he was off again, scribbling down a note and calling for Mrs. Hudson to fetch someone to send off a telegram. He then turned his gaze to the rainy streets below, thrust his hands deep into the pockets of his dressing gown, and stared wistfully into space for what seemed an interminable period of time.

I had grown accustomed to Holmes's erratic behavior by this time, but I was never not in awe of the frenetic changes which accompanied his mercurial temperament. Oscillating constantly between extremes of energy and lethargy, Holmes could not be doing his constitution any favors and there were occasions when I feared for his well-being, but I had learned to keep my remonstrations to myself, or else he would scold me for worrying over him like a mother would her child.

An answer came to his telegram at length and he tore open the message anxiously reading it twice over before he turned to me beaming.

"How would you feel about braving the elements, my dear Watson, and paying a visit to Mrs. Cornelia Willis?"

The name did not immediately strike my ears as familiar, but I remembered in short order that she was the woman who had introduced Thomas Fraser to the painter, Neville Devlin.

"If you think that her opinion will yield answers, then I should be happy to accompany you."

Holmes grinned wryly. "Capital! Allow me a moment to change and we shall be off."

True to his word, Holmes was ready in nearly no time at all, and we were soon trundling through the conspicuously empty city towards an address in Belgravia.

"Mrs. Willis's was a name which featured regularly in the society pages where the Frasers were concerned," Holmes said by way of explanation as we were ensconced in the belly of a hansom cab. "I sent her a message requesting the opportunity to speak and to put to her a few questions about the couple. It occurred to me, Watson, that we know only the Frasers as portrayed in the pages of the society columns. They are merely a caricature. Who better to fill in the gaps than one of their closest friends?"

"But surely Thomas Fraser proved himself to be the genuine article this morning?"

"Ah, but to question everything is one of the hallmarks of my profession," Holmes retorted. "We can never truly know what really lies behind Fraser's eyes."

Our cab drew up before an elegantly appointed stone house; one which stood in a row of a number of nearly identical-looking stone edifices situated on a narrow but prosperous section of road. Holmes had hardly approached the front door before it was opened from within by a jubilant-looking woman of about thirty. Her freckled face and auburn hair were quite pretty to behold, and I confess I did find myself turning a light shade of red as she shook my hand enthusiastically to compliment me upon my account of Holmes's work. She gestured for us to follow her into the sitting room which we did and found a service of tea set out welcoming us. I in turn had to compliment Mrs. Willis on her forethought as a hostess.

"Living the life I do, one is expected to provide for one's guests. Your thanks are quite unnecessary, Doctor."

Holmes declined the offer of tea and also refused to sit, instead electing to make a circuit around the elegant room, admiring a portrait of a young woman – no older than our hostess – which hung on the wall opposite the fire.

"This is quite an exquisite painting," he said. "Whose portrait is it?"

"Ah," Mrs. Willis said, taking a sip from her cup of tea, "that would be Amelia. Amelia Fitzroy. God rest her soul."

"My condolences," I said. Mrs. Willis turned her rueful gaze to me and murmured a hushed word of thanks.

"This painting seems to be a new addition to the room," Holmes said. "Was Mrs. Fitzroy's death a recent one?"

"She died a year ago. The poor thing had never been in great health and I am afraid that she shuffled off this mortal coil last spring. It is hard to cope with the loss of any person, Mr. Holmes, but to lose one whom you considered your very best of friends is even harder."

"Of course," Holmes replied. "I am sure that she would be quite happy that her memory lives on within these walls in this portrait. The artist did a remarkable job in capturing the subject's image."

"Ah, that's Neville's handiwork. The man is a genius."

Holmes turned sharply on his heel. "Neville Devlin?"

Cornelia Willis nodded wordlessly and sipped at her tea. "Mr. Devlin is another close of friend of mine. In fact, it was at a party of mine that I introduced him to Thomas Fraser. I believe, Mr. Holmes, that it is he whom you wished to discuss this evening?"

Holmes flashed a grin. "Yes, you will forgive my distraction, Mrs. Willis, but I do consider myself something of an appreciator of art, and I could not help but find my attention attracted wholly to that portrait."

"Neville would find that quite a compliment, indeed."

Holmes took a seat opposite our hostess. "From what I understand, Mrs. Willis," he began, "you are on quite intimate terms with both Thomas and Lucy Fraser?"

"Indeed I am," she replied. "I consider both some of the closest friends I have."

"Thomas Fraser...he is a good man, especially when one considers the position he is in with his wife as ill as she is."

"Yes, he is indeed a strong man. A saint among men."

Sherlock Holmes flashed a grin. Suddenly he was standing once more. "You will excuse Dr. Watson and me, Mrs. Willis. We have another engagement which simply cannot be broken. But I thank you for your assistance and I am sure that the doctor appreciates your tea."

Holmes wordlessly withdrew from the room leaving me having to not only apologize for his rudeness, but to thank Mrs. Willis once more for her hospitality. I found Holmes standing outside hailing another hansom. Once we were inside, I turned a penetrating glare in his direction to which Holmes did little more than guffaw.

"You will forgive me, Watson, but I found out everything that I wanted to learn from Mrs. Willis in our short visit with her."

"What could you have possibly learned in so short a time?"

"That her relationship with Thomas Fraser goes much deeper than she would have us believe," Holmes began. "And what is more, we have another name to add to our ever-growing list of concerned parties: Amelia Fitzroy."

"The woman in the portrait?"

"Precisely," Holmes replied. "I think that there is little we can do until tomorrow at this rate, Watson, so let us return to Baker Street and head out early tomorrow and have a few words with Mr. Neville Devlin. I believe that a visit with that gentleman shall be quite illuminating."

"We are all endowed with our own tics and tells, my dear fellow," said Sherlock Holmes as we sat in a closed carriage the following morning on our way to visit the illustrious Mr. Neville Devlin. Holmes was explaining to me – at last! – his words from the previous evening concerning the relationship between Thomas Fraser and Cornelia Willis. As was his habit, Holmes refused to divulge more information than was necessary, but this had left me totally clueless and fuming as a result. Seeing my attitude the following morning – the tumultuous rain of the previous day having given way to a sunnier and cheerier spring day – I do believe that my friend elected to break from his habit and share his thoughts as we trundled once more through the metropolis.

"One merely has to study these things," he continued, "not unlike how a card player reads the minute, almost imperceptible actions of his fellow players. I read Mrs. Willis in much the same way when we visited with her last evening."

"But I was watching her just as you were, Holmes, what could you have seen that I did not?"

Holmes grinned mischievously. "I saw you observing her, my dear fellow. Should I speak objectively, I would say that Mrs. Willis is quite an attractive young woman. However, that is entirely beside the point. As I said, those signals are there, but unless you were looking for them, I doubt that you would notice. You surely were not paying much mind to Mrs. Willis' grasp on her tea cup and saucer?"

I shook my head negatively.

"As soon as she brought up Thomas Fraser, her hand began to quiver ever so slightly, as though the mention of the name arouses for her great emotion. And – as we continued to speak on the young couple – I noticed Mrs. Willis's eyes begin to dilate. I sat close enough that I could observe her closely in this way and these two factors led me to believe that Mrs. Willis harbors great romantic feelings for the solicitor. I would be very surprised, indeed, should those feelings go unrequited."

"But you saw how concerned he is for his wife!" I said. "The man was very nearly in tears when he called upon you yesterday."

"Surely this is an ordeal for him," Holmes retorted, "but could those tears not also come from the extreme guilt which he feels for finding solace in the arms of another woman? I pose the question rhetorically, Watson, but it is one which I would not discount at this time. Ah, but here we are. Let us put a few questions to Mr. Devlin."

Our cab had drawn up before a tall stone building on The Strand; Holmes alighting and making for the door, rapping upon it with the head of his stick. I joined him a moment later just as the door was being opened from within by a youngish man dressed in his shirtsleeves. He was a handsome gentleman from his dark green eyes to his head of black hair, one curl of which lay upon his forehead. He smiled a thin-lipped grin as he answered the door; a grin which seemed to apologize for not looking his most presentable.

"Mr. Neville Devlin?" Holmes inquired. The man nodded in greeting. "My name is Sherlock Holmes. I would like to talk to you about Thomas and Lucy Fraser."

Devlin's grin faded at the mention of the name. "Ah, poor thing," he said. "Dear, dear Lucy. Come in, gentlemen, please."

We entered into a low, but comfortable foyer appointed with a few still-life paintings, works which I guessed were originals. Holmes shook hands with the artist and introduced me in turn. I took Devlin's hand – a rough hand which was not entirely free from dabs of paint between his fingers. I marveled for an instant that those hands could be so dexterous and have given life to works which were revered the city over.

"I should very much like to see your studio, Mr. Devlin," Holmes said, "if you are willing to show off your *sanctum sanctorum* to two relative strangers."

"It would be my honor, gentlemen," Devlin replied. "I have followed accounts of your work with keen interest, Mr. Holmes. To have such a celebrity in my own home is thrilling. Please, follow me."

Devlin led us to a spiral staircase which crept up to the third floor of the building. As we climbed, Holmes's hawk-like head swiveled from side to side taking in every detail of his surroundings.

"I dread to think of how Mrs. Lucy Fraser fared on this staircase during each one of her visits," he said.

"Yes," Devlin replied over his shoulder. "Poor Lucy was never in good health when she sat for me, but she also insisted upon climbing up here – often under her own power too. I knew that it caused Thomas some great duress, but I hoped that the finished portrait would bring some happiness into her life."

An uncomfortable quiet settled over us until we had reached the top of the stairs and stepped into Devlin's studio. The whole of the space was occupied by his work; a vacant stool sitting on one end of the room on which his subject would surely sit, while an empty easel was situated on the opposite end of the long room. Cabinets and shelves full bursting with such paraphernalia that I can only guess at lined the walls and, looking up, I saw that much of the ceiling was made up of a large glass window. The whole place was a veritable shrine to Devlin's artistic endeavors, and I wondered just how god-like the man must have felt bringing life to works each day while the heavens looked down upon him.

"This is a most impressive set-up, Mr. Devlin," Holmes said as he paced around the room, his hands clasped behind his back. "Should I be as artistically inclined as you, I should be just a bit envious."

Devlin laughed and waved away the notion with his hand. "The space in which one does his work is of little consequence," he said. "It's the work itself which truly matters."

"From what I have heard of your work, it is of the highest order as well," I said.

"Ah, my blushes, Dr. Watson."

"I should very much like to see your portrait of Lucy Fraser," Holmes said. "Do you still have it?"

Devlin grinned. "It is, of course, no longer the masterwork it once was, but I hold on to it yet as a reminder of this whole queer business."

He produced from his pocket a ring of keys and gestured for us to follow him to a low door at the opposite end of the chamber. Inserting it into a lock, he pulled open the door to a small antechamber into which we stepped. The room was dimly lit but as my eyes adjusted to the low light I could divine five completed portraits; each one featuring a young woman dressed in her finery, each painted in the same careful hand which captured a remarkable likeness of the subject. I recognized at once the same handiwork of the man who had painted the late Amelia Fitzroy whose portrait hung in the home of Mrs. Cornelia Willis.

However, what truly grabbed my attention was the final portrait which stood in this row. It too featured a well-dressed young subject, but where a woman's face would surely have once been, there was nothing more than a gaping hole. Staring through the canvas at the back wall of the room was rather disquieting and I inexplicably felt a cold chill pass down my spine upon looking at it. I was very nearly unaware that I had verbalized, "What a pity" until after I had spoken the words aloud.

"I thought so too, doctor," Devlin said turning to me. "One puts his heart and soul into a work like that and to see it desecrated so…it was surely not easy."

Holmes stepped forward, scrutinizing the painting further. "Do you believe Mrs. Fraser to be of unsound mind, Mr. Devlin?"

"I don't think it's my place to say, Mr. Holmes," the artist replied.

Holmes turned on his heel. "Quite right, Mr. Devlin. I would never think to put words in your mouth."

"Nothing to worry over," Devlin replied. "If you could tell me, sir – I left my watch in my room downstairs – what is the time?"

Holmes took his watch from his waistcoat pocket. "It is very nearly eleven now."

"I would never think of rushing you gentlemen along, but I do have another subject coming in soon. If you will excuse me, I will just go and put on a pot of tea. Please, gentlemen, examine the paintings as long as you'd like."

I watched as Devlin disappeared down the stairs the way we had come, leaving Holmes and I to stare at his works in silence. My friend did nothing to break the quiet, instead he looked at each of the artist's past successes with keen interest, drawing himself up close to each canvas and inspecting it with his customary thoroughness. He seemed to be broken from his reverie only when Devlin returned a few moments later carrying a tray on which he carried a full service.

"Do you always make your subjects tea, Mr. Devlin?"

The artist grinned. "Always. It's part of my prerogative. I find that it not only relaxes those of a more nervous disposition, but can also energize those of a more mellow outlook. I find that it's best to have subjects who are just as excited to sit for you as you are to paint them."

"Of course," Holmes said. "As an artist you, no doubt, feed off the creative energy of anyone who observes your craft."

"Precisely, Mr. Holmes. If Dr. Watson's account is to be believed, you are something of an artist yourself? A violin player?"

Holmes batted away the suggestion with a wave of his hand. "I am hardly an artist, Mr. Devlin, even if I have fooled myself into believing so in some flight of fancy. But, we have occupied enough of your time already and the good doctor and I have a great deal of work to tend to today. My many thanks for letting us visit."

Holmes went to gather his hat and stick from where he had deposited them on the breakfast table when we had first arrived in Devlin's studio and, as he gathered them up, turning to go he bumped into Devlin, knocking the tea service from the man's grasp. The whole tray fell to the floor, china scattering in all directions as the hot tea oozed from the broken pot.

"Oh, good heavens!" Holmes cried. "How clumsy of me. A thousand apologies, Mr. Devlin."

Devlin had grabbed for a towel and was already crouching on his hands and knees to mop up the spilled drink.

"You needn't apologize, Mr. Holmes," he said. "Accidents do happen."

"Please," said Holmes withdrawing his card from his inner pocket, "I insist on paying for the damages. If, in the next few days you are able to buy a new tea service, I insist that you send the bill my way. A shop which specializes in knick-knacks and bric-a-brac in Covent Garden is familiar with me. If you purchase it there, I am sure that the proprietor will only be too happy to turn the matter over to me."

"You are too kind, Mr. Holmes. My many thanks."

Holmes smiled and tipped his hat before descending the stairs and out of the building. I followed closely behind and, once we were standing out on the street once more, Holmes suddenly changed his demeanor entirely. The polite façade which he had erected and employed before Devlin only moments ago had vanished completely and he was hailing a cab, deep concentration etched on his face. Once we had climbed inside, he at last spoke:

"We are dealing with a monster, Watson."

"Good God," I said. "You mean Devlin?"

Holmes nodded silently.

"But I don't understand," I replied lamely. "He seemed like such a nice chap. I cannot imagine why –"

"Ah," said Holmes lifting his index to silence me, "remember the words of the Bard: 'One may smile, and smile, and be a villain.' And what a villain Neville Devlin is! I daresay, Watson, in our many years together, we have seldom faced a foe as dangerous – and as coy – as he. The man confessed his crimes to us – indeed he has confessed to countless others – and no one has done anything to stop him."

"I admit that I am utterly lost," I replied.

"You shall see soon enough, Watson," the detective replied, his fingers drumming on the head of his stick in his habitual nervous manner. "I must return to Baker Street immediately and send off a telegram to Lestrade. I am sure that once he has been informed of the truth that the inspector shall have no qualms about going and arresting Devlin."

"Arrest him? But what for, man?"

"For murder, Watson. For calculated and cunning murder."

My blood froze as Holmes spoke, my mind a blur as we raced back towards Baker Street. When we drew up outside our flat, Holmes sprang out leaving me to handle the fare and charge after him. By the time that I had climbed the steps to our sitting room, he was already hard at work, having pounced upon his index once more and was rifling through newspaper clippings. I stood back silently knowing that it was best to leave him to his work, and he was thusly occupied for nearly an hour. In that time he spoke not a word to me, instead he murmured in sharp, hushed tones to himself as he selected sheets from his pile, plucking at them with his nervous fingers. He had accumulated something of a pile of clippings at the end of the hour and seemingly satisfied with his work, dashed off a telegram to Inspector Lestrade urging him to drop everything and come to Baker Street posthaste.

It seemed as though the inspector heeded Holmes's words for he had arrived in something of a frenzied state within the hour.

"What is it that is so important, Mr. Holmes? You were cryptic – as usual – in your telegram."

Holmes gestured for the inspector to sit and, once he had perched himself on the edge of the settee, Holmes pressed the small pile of newspaper clippings into his hand. "These artists' renderings should be enough to put the noose around the neck of Mr. Neville Devlin."

Lestrade looked at the clippings in turn. "Six women," he said. "I see no connection."

"Ostensibly, those six women are only tenuously linked. Each comes from a well-to-do section of the city and has probably rubbed elbows with each other, but aside from that I believe that they are only united by one factor: they had their portraits painted by Neville Devlin before their untimely deaths. According to the obituaries of those six women, each one suffered from a similar wasting disease in their final days – not unlike the disease which is currently ravaging Mrs. Lucy Fraser, Devlin's intended seventh victim."

"Mr. Holmes," said Lestrade, "I think you ought to start from the beginning. I'm lost in all of this."

Holmes huffed as though irritated that the inspector – and for that matter myself – had not grasped the full meaning of his words. "Neville Devlin is a renowned artist," he began, "who, as we have learned, has painted stunning portraits of London's elite. Those portraits are still to be found in his studio in The Strand. Why should he keep these paintings for himself: their owners are no longer alive to claim them. In fact, they were murdered by Devlin; poisoned even as he immortalized them in oils. The only portrait which we know of Devlin's to have been released from his studio is that which currently belongs to Mrs. Cornelia Willis, and that was of her late friend, Amelia Fitzroy.

"Devlin is a fiend, and nothing less, inspector. His method of murder is a simple and nearly untraceable one, lacing his subjects' tea with poison – just enough to render them weak and infirm for weeks at a time, and continuing to do so on each occasion that they visit him. The portrait – surely as good as a confession as it is the only thing which binds each of the women together – is his memento of their passing; rendering each painting's exquisite beauty instead a showcase for Devlin's disturbed brain."

"But what of Lucy Fraser?" I asked.

"No doubt she had a revelation," Holmes replied. "I am sure that she could see that her illness was driving her husband away from her, and she no doubt took solace in the arms of the only man who would pay her any mind: Devlin. Why else should we insist through all the weakness, all the pain which she experienced to have her portrait completed? However, when the portrait was completed she knew that her time on earth was short. Doubtless, Lucy Fraser had divined the link between Devlin's six previous victims and knew that her completed portrait meant that her death was imminent. Her heart, however, won out and – attempting to shield the man whom she inexplicably fell in love with – she took up a knife from his breakfast table and obscured her face. No one would be able to identify the seventh woman in Devlin's portrait series and nothing would link her own untimely passing to the others'."

"It's horrible," I gasped, "utterly unthinkable."

"I can only hope that I have prevented another casualty this very day," Holmes continued, "by breaking Devlin's tea service. Perhaps I have saved someone from Devlin's weekly dose of death."

Holmes acknowledged that his theory stood, presently, on conjecture, but Lestrade was able to secure a warrant for Devlin's arrest that very evening. Upon inspection of his studio, Lestrade found arsenic in Devlin's possession and a confession – one totally without remorse and filled with gloating condescension – was shortly forthcoming. I, the following day, tended to Lucy Fraser personally and, with instructions to her personal physician, was able to begin the process of bringing the poor woman back to health.

It seemed that the dreadful business had come to a close. That is until one afternoon nearly a week later when I returned to Baker Street from a walk to find that Thomas Fraser was standing in our sitting room. Holmes was seated in his chair, pulling contentedly on his pipe.

"You shall be glad to hear, doctor," said Holmes as I entered and closed the door behind me, "that Lucy Fraser is already beginning to show signs of improvement."

"I'm certainly glad to hear it."

"She is still not yet strong and she may never be again," Fraser said. "That devil Devlin used Lucy's already weak constitution as a mask for his scheme, it seems, but she is on the mend."

"So it would appear," said Holmes, rising from his seat. "My thanks for keeping me abreast of your wife's recovery, Mr. Fraser. Do keep me informed."

Holmes shook hands with the solicitor. "And one word of warning to you, sir," Holmes said as Fraser turned to his back to go. "Keep your eyes to your wife alone. Many a man has been tempted by the forbidden fruit of Eden, but you must consider the consequence. Traversing the rocky precipice of love is a dangerous prospect. Take care that you do not slip. Mr. Fraser, have a good afternoon."

The Adventure of the
Traveling Corpse

One evening in the early spring of 1890, Sherlock Holmes and I decided to walk back from the opera finding the warm weather inviting for the time of year. Holmes was in a cheerful mood – much to my relief – and we had taken to spending time together at the end of each week. Having moved out of our Baker Street digs, I made a conscious effort to see more of my old friend and – with my wife visiting friends in the country – I reasoned that tonight would be a perfect opportunity to take my friend up on his offer of visiting the opera and taking in a show.

As we made our way towards Baker Street, I could hear Holmes hum the music under his breath almost note-for-note. His uncanny ability for mental processing was unparalleled in any other man I have known. Rounding the corner onto Baker Street, I was about to make mention of the fact when he stopped dead in his tracks and pointed towards our rooms with his stick.

"The light is on," he said.

"Is that so curious?" I asked. "Perhaps Mrs. Hudson is tidying up, or perhaps Billy is going about doing a few errands?"

"Possible," Holmes replied, "but unlikely. Our landlady is a creature of habit and with it being nearly nine now, I am sure that she is recessed in the kitchenette as she always is this time of night. As for Billy, the young boy's off in the country visiting an aunt. He left early this morning. No, my dear Watson, the light emanating from our sitting room can mean only one thing."

"A client?" I asked.

"A client! Come; let us not keep him waiting for much longer!"

Practically sprinting the rest of the way, Holmes opened the front door and stepped into the foyer with the zeal of a truly determined man. Preparing to ascend the stairs to the sitting room, his attention and mine were arrested by Mrs. Hudson who came bustling out of the kitchen.

"There's a woman upstairs to see you, Mr. Holmes," she said.

"Yes, Mrs. Hudson," Holmes said. "I could see the light from the street. Thank you for showing her up."

"She seemed most insistent upon seeing you," our landlady replied.

A grin crossed Holmes's stern face. "Excellent. Come along Doctor. I value your assistance greatly."

Following Holmes up the stairs, I entered behind him as he flung open the door to our rooms with flair. Removing his top hat and gloves, he strode into the room as I closed the door behind him. Our client was a rotund, red-faced woman in her early fifties. She was well-dressed but a look of absolute disbelief and horror had crossed her face.

"Good evening madam," said Holmes, "I am Sherlock Holmes and this is my friend and colleague, Dr. John Watson."

The woman had almost jumped from her seat upon our entering and Holmes had to ease her back onto the sofa.

"You are obviously distressed, madam," he said. "I shall endeavor to help you."

Holmes eased himself into his chair. "I see that you have just come in on the 8.12 from Birmingham."

"Yes," the woman sputtered. "How on earth did you know that?"

Holmes waved his hand dismissively. "I observed the upper part of a train ticket protruding from your glove. I also find that it is quite invaluable to have an in-depth knowledge of the London train schedule and judging by your presence here and your flushed appearance I should judge that whatever has brought you to my doorstep happened very recently – perhaps just after your arrival in the city. Therefore, your train just recently arrived. The 8.12 seemed like the most likely option then."

"Well, that's splendid," she said. "Absolutely splendid."

"Quite commonplace, madam," Holmes replied. "Now then, please lay all of the facts of your case before me."

He sat back in his seat and placed his fingertips together before his face.

"Well," the woman began, "I suppose I ought to begin by letting you know just who I am. My name is Louisa McGinty and – just as you said – I live in Birmingham. I have only been to London a handful of times in my life, Mr. Holmes, but if what happened to be me this evening is anything to go by then I cannot say that I shall be returning anytime soon.

"Well, I have two children. They have gone off and made their way in the world, both of them moving to London. I lived then with my husband until his death last year and, finding myself alone, I was invited down here for a weekend with them. I am not fond of uprooting myself, but the prospect of seeing them both again was something I could not pass up and decided upon it. So, I bought my ticket and made arrangements to stay with my son in Piccadilly Circus. I boarded the train and arrived precisely on time at Euston Station.

"By some misfortune my son – and my daughter for that matter – were indisposed this evening, and he was unable to collect me at the station. I was therefore on my own in this strange city and found myself unable to catch a cab from the station. So, not knowing how far of a walk it was, I decided that I'd start off on foot and hopefully run across someone who might be able to tell me how to get to Piccadilly Circus, or perhaps even better to find a cabbie willing to drive me there.

"I had gone a few blocks and had entered a residential neighborhood. I fear that the street name has escaped me completely but it was a fashionable part of town. Despite the nicety of the vicinity,

I couldn't help but feel a little unnerved by it all. I was alone in this city with little idea of where to go. And then, as if all of my prayers were answered, I saw a hansom at the end of the street. I started towards it and…well Mr. Holmes, that's when it happened."

"When *what* happened, Mrs. McGinty?"

"From one of the houses, I saw two men exit. They appeared to be carrying a large object but, as I drew closer, I could tell distinctly that it was a body! I stopped dead in my tracks for fear that the duo would see me but they seemed too occupied in their present endeavor. Together, they hoisted the body into the hansom and while one man jumped inside as well, the other took up the reins, cracked the whip and the cab disappeared into the night.

"Well, reasonably enough I was at my wit's end, Mr. Holmes. With little notion what to do, I hurried back the way I had come. I needed help at once and, fearing that the police might laugh at my story – I am after all a dotty old woman from the country not used to life in the city – I remembered hearing of your name, Mr. Holmes. I managed to find a cabbie and asking for 221b Baker Street, I arrived on your doorstep."

The woman drew in a deep breath as she concluded her story.

"Remarkable," I said. "It's utterly fantastic."

"That is how I feared that Scotland Yard would react," Mrs. McGinty replied. "Though I am sure that the police take all cases of murder seriously, I feared the possible ridicule which might come with this outlandish tale of mine."

"There is nothing outlandish about your story, Mrs. McGinty," Holmes replied. "In fact I am certain that your case ought to be handled with the utmost sincerity. I am more than happy to take on your case but I require one or two things from you."

"Certainly, Mr. Holmes."

"You say that you had no idea what street or neighborhood you found yourself on when you witnessed the men disposing of the corpse," Holmes said, "but do you believe that you would be able to retrace your steps from Euston Station?"

"I really couldn't say, Mr. Holmes," Mrs. McGinty replied. "I could certainly try but it was dark and I have never been good with direction."

"Do you think that you would recognize the street should you find yourself on it again?"

"That question I do believe I can answer in the affirmative."

Holmes grinned. "Excellent. One last question, though I fear it is a long shot: did you happen to see the number of the hansom which the two men climbed into?"

"I'm afraid not, Mr. Holmes."

"Ah, no matter Mrs. McGinty," Holmes said. "Now then, seeing as this is a matter of murder, I cannot in good conscience keep this from the police, bumbling as they may be. However, if you feel that your unfamiliarity with the city will color the impressions of the Metropolitan Police's finest than I shall bring the matter to them myself. However, I shall need your son's address in Piccadilly Circus should they need to contact you."

Mrs. McGinty provided Holmes with her son's address. Scribbling it on his shirt cuff, he thanked her and opened the door wide.

"Perhaps, Watson," he said, "you could procure for Mrs. McGinty a cab so she needn't search the city aimlessly for another."

I ventured down into the street with our client and after seeing her off in a hansom, returned to our sitting room where Holmes was pouring us both drinks from the sideboard.

"Thoughts, Doctor?" he asked as he pressed a glass into my hand. I slid into my chair before the fire and reached for my cigarette case.

"It's quite an extraordinary case," I said. "To think that the murderers would be brazen enough to dispose of the corpse on a city street...in a hansom! It's fantastic!"

"Indeed," my friend murmured. "The case is a unique one and, I fear, it may prove to be quite challenging. Unfortunately for us – and the police – Mrs. McGinty is unable to name the street where the whole thing happened."

"Then how shall you go about looking into the matter?"

"We may be in for a challenge, my dear Watson," Holmes said, "but I very much doubt that the case is hopeless. I shall begin with a very detailed perusal of the newspapers tomorrow morning."

"Looking for what?"

"Anything. Anything at all. If something strikes my fancy then I very much think it ought to be scrutinized and examined in depth. I wager that you shall want a hand in the investigation, my friend?"

"Certainly," I said. "That is if I can be of any assistance."

"My dear Watson," Holmes said, "you do yourself a disservice and I daresay you habitually underrate your own abilities. Tomorrow morning shall be spent in full pursuit of facts from the printed word."

I quit Baker Street not long afterward. Arriving home I drifted off to sleep easily and, waking myself early, I ate a simple breakfast before hurrying back to Baker Street despite the heavy rain which came with the warm weather. Once inside the familiar brick building once more, I hadn't even started up the stairs when I knew that my friend had already begun the hunt. His goulashes – saturated with mud and rain – were standing in the foyer. Ascending the steps to the sitting room, I eased open the door and found Holmes seated upon the hearthrug, one leg crossed over the other, as he perused at least half-a-dozen newspapers which were spread out before him; analyzing each one over the stem of his cherrywood pipe.

"Ah, Watson," he said as I entered, "good of you to come 'round early. I have already begun the search."

"I can see," I said smugly, "though I knew that before I had ever set foot in this room."

"Oh? And how did you know that?"

"Simple," I said. "I observed your goulashes drenched in mud and water in the foyer downstairs."

Sherlock Holmes laughed heartily. "A simple observation but accurate all-the-same. Come. I have laid aside a few papers for you to read. Do not overlook anything which may seem of interest to us."

We spent the remainder of the morning in virtual silence. I scanned columns and columns of text while Holmes did the same. After nearly an hour however, he stood and rummaged through his bookshelf until he found a large map of London which he spread out on the breakfast table and scrutinized with the same intensive glare which he had given to the periodicals.

With the clock about to chime noon, I stood and poured myself a drink. "Anything?" I asked Holmes at length.

"I rather think so," he replied. He pointed with the stem of his pipe at a point on the map. "These streets here seem to me to be the most likely streets on which Mrs. Louisa McGinty found herself last evening. Though I cannot at present narrow them down from the current six or seven, I would be thoroughly surprised to learn that she had made it any further than Taviton Street."

"That is in the right direction towards Piccadilly Circus," I said.

"Indeed," Holmes said. "As to any articles of interest in the news, I have a very strong candidate for further investigation but I should like to hear if you have anything worthy of mentioning."

"I fear not," I said. "I do not think that my perusal has been very fruitful. But, what did you find?"

Holmes scooped up *The Times* from the floor. "Only a few lines mind you," he said, "but allow me to read from it."

He cleared his throat. "The headline reads 'Military Man Vanishes.' The article itself runs thus, 'According to the family of Colonel Walter Cunningham, the patriarch of the Cunningham family has vanished without trace. Last seen at his club on Thursday evening, the Colonel seemed to be in high spirits before he headed homeward. It is reported by the Colonel's wife – Mrs. Sophie Cunningham – that her husband was heard returning home late Thursday evening. However, after going to his study, it is believed that he went out again and did not return. A police investigation has been launched.'"

"Extraordinary," I murmured. "You think that the dead man was this Colonel Cunningham?"

"It is, at present, the most likely possibility. I should very much like to speak with the man in charge of the case."

So saying, Holmes scribbled a note upon a sheet of paper and rushing downstairs delivered it into the hands of Mrs. Hudson. Returning a moment later, he bemoaned not being able to do much until his cable was answered and suggested that we confine ourselves to luncheon and take refuge from the tumultuous storm outside.

The answer to Holmes's wire came an hour later. Mrs. Hudson delivered it to Holmes who tore it open zealously. He chuckled as he read it over.

"Well?" I asked.

"The man in charge of the Cunningham investigation is none other than our good friend Inspector Lestrade. Ha! And to think that only this morning while I was out getting these papers I wired Lestrade the details of Mrs. McGinty's case. I shouldn't be very surprised if the good inspector is rather cross with me now as I'm sure he had enough to contend with being knee-deep in his current investigation.

"All-the-same, this is good news for us my friend. With Lestrade heading the case, I imagine that he will be more willing to divulge some further details about the Cunningham case. Would you be adverse to braving this weather and taking a ride to Scotland Yard now?"

Telling Holmes in all seriousness that I would like nothing more, we gathered up our hats and coats and made our way outside. Hailing a cab, we climbed inside and started for Scotland Yard. As we rode together in the hansom, I could see my friend brimming with anticipation. Acting as he did as an independent consulting detective, he was able to work outside of the law. In this way, Holmes could maintain his low opinion of the official police force and, though I have perhaps given readers the wrong impression about them, they truly weren't all that bad. Surely no one would be able to compete with Holmes's mental prowess, but I thought that they did a capable job in their own way. Though their methods were slipshod at times, when acting on more routine matters I couldn't fault the Scotland Yarders in the slightest.

And, I think that Holmes knew this and grew to look down on them as something of a minor jest. Inspectors Lestrade, Gregson, and Jones may have grated upon him, but he knew that they were not a bad lot.

Disembarking from our carriage, Holmes pressed a coin into the cabbie's hand and we made our way to Inspector Lestrade's small office located on the third floor.

"Well, well, Mr. Holmes," he said as we entered his office, "come to offer me another case?"

"No," my friend replied. "I would very much like some information."

"*Information*? What about?"

"The Cunningham case," Holmes said. "You are the man in charge of the investigation and, though I hesitate to say anything definite, I would be surprised in the extreme to learn that the Colonel's disappearance is not linked to Mrs. Louisa McGinty's testimony."

"You mean to say that the two mysterious men seen stowing a body into a hansom cab were disposing of the Colonel's body?"

"As I said Lestrade, I would be surprised in the extreme if that were otherwise."

Seeming to finally register what an impact this would have on his case, Lestrade took a seat behind his desk ready to lay out all of the facts to us.

"Well, it's like this, Mr. Holmes; Colonel Walter Cunningham was something of a notable figure in Her Majesty's military. Had you ever heard of him?"

"I defer all military knowledge to the doctor," Holmes replied.

"Doctor?"

"Thinking on it now," I said, "I think I have heard the name connected with the Boer War."

"Indeed Dr. Watson," Lestrade said. "Colonel Cunningham gained notoriety for his service to Queen and country in that war and in that time since his return from the front, he has amassed something of a family...and wealth. The woman to whom he is now married, Sophie Cunningham, is in fact his second wife and she is some fifteen years his junior. I am no expert in societal news, Mr. Holmes, but I do believe that there are some who believed that she had married him merely for the notoriety and the money which came with his estate. She is also an actress which has colored many people's opinion of her.

"All-the-same, the Colonel, a frequenter of a club in Pall Mall, was in good spirits when he left the club on Thursday night. According to the other members, Cunningham did not drink nor did he smoke, and he seemed to be in full possession of his faculties when he left. He was seen off by the doorman of the club and he turned up at home sometime before eleven according to both Mrs. Cunningham (I'll get back to her in a moment), and the Colonel's military batman – and his butler – a man called Mathews.

"According to Mathews, the Colonel arrived home and insisted that he had some work to tend to before he retired to bed. The Colonel then went off to his study and locked himself in. This story is verified by Mrs. Cunningham who said that she retired to bed with a slight headache earlier in the evening. However, with the door to her bedroom ajar she could hear her husband enter the house and exchange words with Mathews.

"Only fifteen minutes or so elapsed before the Colonel remerged from his study and said that he had to go back out. Mathews said that he saw the Colonel hail another cab, climb inside, and drive away and he has not been seen since."

"If Cunningham were the dead man," Holmes said, "that leaves nearly an entire day unaccounted for. In that time the Colonel had to disappear, be killed, and end up on the other side of the city in order to be loaded into a cab."

"Are you starting to doubt your theory, Mr. Holmes?"

"No," the detective replied. "I am merely trying to put things into a sequence. I find that putting things into a proper order is beneficial in the extreme. Now, Inspector, what do you think of Mrs. Cunningham? Do you take her to be the conniving social-climber that she is made out to be?"

"I really couldn't say, Mr. Holmes," Lestrade said. "She seemed to be quite a genuine, concerned young woman when I spoke to her."

"The Colonel's family," I interjected, "what of them?"

"They're quite estranged," Lestrade replied. "When the Colonel's first wife died some four years ago and he married his second wife, I believe that did divide the family. As it stands, however, the Colonel has two sons. They, as I discovered, were both out of the city at the time of their father's disappearance. Indeed, until I did some digging I doubt that they had even heard about their father's disappearance."

Holmes seemed to be staring into space absorbing all of the information. "Inspector," he said at length, "do you think it would be possible for Dr. Watson and me to examine Cunningham's house?"

"I do not see why not," Lestrade said.

"Excellent," Holmes said standing. "Then I think that no time would suit that endeavor better than the present." He started to go when he whirled about on his heel. "And one other matter, Lestrade: have you spoken to Cunningham's solicitor?"

"I have. Why?"

"In the event of the Colonel's death, what happens to that wealth which he has accumulated?"

"According to the solicitor, Cunningham's home is passed onto his wife. The residue of his estate would then be divided amongst his two sons and, rather curiously, Mathews the butler."

Holmes tapped a long finger on his lips. "Curious," I heard him murmur. "Very well, Lestrade. Dr. Watson and I shall be waiting downstairs."

While we waited for the inspector, Holmes lighted a cigarette and continued to stare into space lost in thought.

"Do you suppose that Mrs. Cunningham and Mathews knew about their share of the Colonel's wealth?" I asked.

"Possibly," Holmes replied. "In my experience men like Colonel Cunningham are not tight-lipped when it comes to their affairs. What's more, you must consider the character of the people with whom he was dividing his monetary gains. One is his wife; the woman he dotes on without doubt. She is, after all, the only woman in his life after the death of his first wife. Then there is Mathews, the butler. Serving as he did with Mathews during the Boer War, the two men are quite close. You ought to understand that, my dear fellow."

"You're correct, Holmes," I said. "I am still inclined to write to my orderly, Murray."

"Precisely," Holmes said. "I would be more surprised than anything else if I learned that Mrs. Cunningham and Mathews were in the dark concerning the amount of money they had coming to them in the event of the Colonel's death. And, with the Colonel's estate being worth what it was, I am certain that any man or woman would play quite a bold game in order to get his or her hands on what they think they deserve."

"But tell me, Holmes; if Cunningham is the victim in all of this, then why go to all of the trouble of carting his body all the way across the city only to load it up into a cab and drive off with it again?"

"It is a fair question, Watson and first thing tomorrow I shall begin a line of enquiry regarding that cab. I think that this is a job for the Baker Street Irregulars."

I rolled my eyes. I did not look forward to Holmes's band of ragamuffins invading our sitting room as they so often did whenever he employed them on a case.

Inspector Lestrade joined us a moment later and together we set off towards Colonel's Cunningham's house.

Our cab ride culminated in our drawing up before a large stone edifice done over in ivy. The place looked romantic and Gothic and, ringing the bell, Lestrade's call was answered almost at once by the butler. Drawing us into the foyer, the man – presumably Mathews – relieved us of our hats and coats.

"Do you have any questions to pose to Mathews, Mr. Holmes?" Lestrade asked.

"Not at present," my friend replied. "I should very much like to examine the Colonel's study."

We proceeded down corridor to the back of the house. Mathews opened the door for us and we drew into the room. At once, Holmes was snooping around the room like a bloodhound trying to pick up the scent. He rushed to the Colonel's desk and rummaged through drawers with incredible tenacity. His search of the desk seemed as if it were at an end when he stopped suddenly a look of surprise entering his grey eyes.

"According to the members of the Colonel's club he had no vices for he did not drink or smoke?"

"That is correct, Mr. Holmes," Lestrade replied. "Why?"

From the bowels of the large oaken desk, Holmes withdrew a small, neat case. I looked it over from a distance and did not at first register what it could possibly be until Holmes undid a clasp on the case. Opening it, I stared at a hypodermic syringe and a small bottle which undoubtedly contained a liquid solution of cocaine. I was taken aback at once.

"Good God," Lestrade said. "The Colonel was a drug addict."

"It very much looks that way," Holmes said. "And, unless I am very much mistaken, the seal which is embossed on this case as well as the bottle belongs to a den in the East End which is habituated by the lowest and vilest cutthroats in this city. My work has taken me to such a place in the past and I number the proprietor amongst my connections in that part of London."

"Perhaps it was this den to which the Colonel flew on the night of his disappearance?" Lestrade suggested.

"It is very possible," Holmes replied. He closed the case and handed it off to Lestrade. He dug around in the drawer for a moment more before he took up a sheet of paper, copied it into a small notebook and then returned the original to the drawer.

"I think that it would be best if we kept this development away from Mrs. Cunningham," Holmes said. "I also think that I have finished my investigation for the time being."

As we made our way out of the study and back towards the foyer, I noticed Holmes stop and cast a glance at a framed portrait on the wall. "I completely failed to notice this," he said. "I assume the man is the Colonel?"

"Of course," Lestrade replied.

Holmes tapped at his lips again. "Most interesting. Ah – Mrs. Cunningham, I presume."

Turning we were all greeted by a youngish, dark-haired woman advancing towards us. I confess that she had a very pretty countenance but I seemed to detect a hint of mischief in her dark, green eyes.

"Inspector Lestrade," she said, "have you made any progress?"

"I think that we have," the inspector replied cryptically. "Ah, allow me to introduce Mr. Sherlock Holmes and his friend and colleague Dr. John Watson."

"How do you do gentlemen?" she asked. "Is there anything that I may do to be of assistance?"

"Not at the moment," Holmes said, "but I would be grateful if you would remain open to cooperating with both me and the inspector."

"Of course," she said. "I will do anything to find out what has happened to my husband."

A thin smile crossed Holmes's face. "Thank you madam," he said. "Dr. Watson and I must take our leave."

Mathews met us at the door and handed us our hats and coats. I saw Holmes study the butler for a moment critically and then, with a smile, tipped his hat at the man and started outside. Lestrade and I followed as he was hailing a cab, the rain having let up since we had left Scotland Yard.

"This case requires some brainwork on my part Lestrade," Holmes said. "I shall be readily available at Baker Street if I am needed." Turning to me Holmes continued. "I fear that I shall be bad company tonight, Watson. This case is a three pipe problem and I know how you detest me poisoning the atmosphere of our rooms. However, if you would be so good as to call around at ten o'clock tomorrow, I suspect that I shall have one or two developments to relate."

"Of course."

The three of us parted ways and I returned home and busied myself for the remainder of the day with some reading. I confess that I was unable to make head nor tail of the whole case, but Holmes seemed to be putting some of the pieces of the puzzle together. He was, as ever, cryptic about the whole thing and would not reveal more to me than the slightest bits of information. His infernal habit of keeping me in the dark could be positively infuriating.

Desperate for answers, I made sure that I called around at Baker Street just as Holmes told me to do the following day. I arrived early and found the room unoccupied. Settling into my chair and lighting a cigarette, I heard a commotion in the hall below and a moment later, a ragged-looking stranger burst into the room. He was a scraggily bearded man with a red face and as he panted, I could see that he had very few teeth remaining in his mouth.

"Good lord," I cried, "what the devil is the meaning of all this?"

"Calm yourself, Watson," the man said in the familiar voice of Sherlock Holmes himself, "please forgive me for my dramatic intrusion. I confess that disguise was hardly my finest –"

"Nonsense! It fooled me rightly enough!"

Holmes chuckled. "Excellent."

He moved to his room where I watched him peel off his beard and bits of the congealed red make-up which he had applied to his cheeks to give himself a realistic, ruddy complexion. He also ran a brush over his teeth and I watched the black substance which he had smeared over them disappear entirely.

"I assume that your disguise aided you in your sojourn to the East End?"

"Precisely," Holmes replied as he sank into his chair and reached for his cigarette case. "I located the den to which I referred yesterday and I made a discovery of unparalleled proportions."

"My goodness Holmes," I said, "out with it! What'd you discover?"

Sherlock Holmes drew in a deep breath. "I found Colonel Walter Cunningham," he said. "He was quite dead. Stabbed through the heart and I should wager anything that he's been dead for two days."

My blood ran cold as Holmes spoke.

"You contacted Lestrade immediately I trust?"

"Of course," my friend replied. He let a thin ring of smoke curl about his head. "The Colonel's body was hauled away to the morgue less than thirty minutes ago. I am sure that the discovery of the corpse in the den was not good business for the proprietor, but that is, I think, rather beside the point."

"I must say Holmes, this does complicate matters. If Colonel Cunningham was a drug addict and he went off to the East End to indulge in his habit on the night of his disappearance, then how could he possibly be in Taviton Street and be seen by Mrs. McGinty? Are you quite certain that the two cases are connected?"

"I am, Watson," Holmes said. "At present I do have a logical chain of events in my mind but it would be remiss of me to elaborate for it is, at present, a very sketchy sequence."

"But can you justify any of this case, Holmes? I must admit, I am lost."

I saw a grin creep across his face. "Perhaps yesterday you saw me scribble down a copy of a note which I found in the Colonel's desk. My brief examination of that note told me that it had arrived in the post that day. The Colonel had obviously tried to hide it away in his desk. The contents of that letter, however, are quite extraordinary."

"What did it say?"

"Very little. The entire note consisted only of a single address: 12 Taviton Street."

"Good heavens," I cried. "So Cunningham *did* go to Taviton Street! Then, he *could* have been the body that Mrs. McGinty saw."

"Yes, Watson. On my way to the drug den this morning, I made a brief pass through that neighborhood. It is a residential neighborhood of the highest order however it should be noted that number twelve is an empty house."

"Surely the writer of that note knew that fact," I said. "Holmes, whoever wrote that was then luring the Colonel to his death."

A pregnant pause fell over the room.

"You know, Watson," Holmes said at length, "there is something curious about Taviton Street. I observed it this morning: the street is almost entirely devoid of streetlamps."

"That's curious," I said. "But, do you think it's significant?"

"I think that it may be one of the most important pieces of information regarding this case. Ah, I do believe that I hear the familiar tread of Inspector Lestrade upon the stair."

Sure enough, a moment later the inspector breathlessly bustled into our rooms.

"Lestrade," Holmes said. "News of the investigation?"

"Yes Mr. Holmes," the inspector replied. "The murderer's flown the nest."

"What?" I cried. "You know who has done this thing?"

"We do, Dr. Watson," Lestrade replied. I cast a glance towards Holmes who seemed just as confused as I was. "It's Mathews," the inspector continued. "He was seen carrying a large valise out of the Colonel's home this morning. One of our men whom I had stationed across the way followed at a distance and saw that Mathews was heading to Charing Cross Station. He's obviously guessed that the Colonel's body has been found and is trying to get away."

"Then," Holmes said standing, "we haven't a moment to lose. If I remember correctly, the next train to depart from Charing Cross is the 11.07 which is in precisely nineteen minutes. Gentlemen, we must make haste."

A few moments later I found myself nestled in a four-wheeler trundling across town; Lestrade having promised the cabbie extra fare if he didn't spare the horse. Holmes's determined face did not betray any of his innermost feelings. Could he, I wondered, have been bested by Lestrade? Could Mathews, the military batman, be the killer?

Our carriage eased to a stop outside of the station and, pressing a coin into the cabbie's hand, Lestrade followed Holmes and me into the busy train terminal.

"It wouldn't do him any good to stay out here," Lestrade said, "he's a wanted man. Perhaps we ought to check the waiting rooms."

"Good idea, inspector," Holmes retorted coldly. "The 11.07 departs for Ipswich so let us head off in that direction."

We started off towards one of the waiting rooms and, as we neared, I could already see the familiar figure of Mathews standing amidst a small throng of people. He clutched his bag to his chest as though he were a mother clutching a newborn baby. He looked nervous, his eyes darting around him. He suddenly locked eyes with Inspector Lestrade who had dug a pair of handcuffs from his inner coat pocket and was rushing forward towards our man. I watched as Mathews dropped his valise to the ground and sprinted off, pushing people aside. By now, Holmes had joined the chase and had rushed to head-off Mathews on the other side of the small crowd. Positioning myself to catch our quarry should he double-back, I lifted my stick ready to strike should I need it.

From across the room, I could see Mathews push aside a couple; the Inspector all but launching himself off the ground to snap the cuffs about the man's wrists. Coming face to face with Holmes, I saw my friend pounce like a tiger but the youthful batman sidestepped Holmes and my friend missed him completely. Recovering beautifully however, Holmes managed to land on his feet, reached out an arm and managed to grab Mathews around the one wrist. Suddenly, Mathews turned on Holmes and his fist collided with my friend's jaw. It was a powerful punch and it managed to fell Sherlock Holmes as if he were a tree.

Seeing Holmes crumble to the ground, I rushed forward even as Lestrade managed to seize our man and snap the handcuffs on him. By the time I reached Holmes he was stirring but his mouth was bloodied from the massive blow he'd received. I withdrew my handkerchief and handed it to Holmes who pressed it to his face. Leaning on me, my friend stood and, taking the handkerchief away from his wound, I saw for the first time how badly injured he had been. The punch which Mathews had inflicted on my friend had knocked from his mouth his left canine altogether. Holmes, who regarded his personal health and safety with a flippancy which did nothing for me as his doctor, waved it away and informed me that he would seek medical attention at once.

"You shall of course place Mathews in police custody, inspector?" he asked Lestrade.

"Of course, Mr. Holmes," the inspector replied. "I shall be very glad to put Colonel Cunningham's murderer behind bars."

"I think then that you shall have to continue looking," Holmes said. "Mathews, here, is not the murderer, of that I am certain. All-the-same, he does play an important part on our drama. Take him to Scotland Yard. Dr. Watson and I shall be around presently. In the meanwhile, I must seek out the aid of a dentist."

I had a friend or two in the dental profession and, showing up on their doorsteps unannounced, I pleaded with them to help my friend. I spent much of the rest of the afternoon at Holmes's side while a specialized doctor looked after his wound and went about making a false tooth for my friend. At the conclusion of the operation, Holmes shook the doctor's hand warmly before stepping out of the office and calling for a cab. Holmes truly could be an automaton and I wordlessly followed him like a loyal dog into the back of a hansom bound for Scotland Yard.

Within the hour, we were seated in a cold, damp room devoid of any color or furniture save or a table which sat in the direct center. Lestrade stood with his arms folded as he leaned against the barred door; Holmes sat in a chair toying with his cigarette case; and Mathews sat, handcuffs still snapped about his wrists, across from the detective.

"You can do nothing but help us, Mathews," Holmes said. "I know that you did not kill Colonel Cunningham, though the evidence against you is overwhelming."

"What motive could I possibly have for killing him?" the manservant cried.

"I think that you were more than just the Colonel's military batman and trusted servant," Holmes said. "You are, in fact, his son."

A silence fell over the room and I exchanged surprised looks with Lestrade.

"It was really obvious to anyone with eyes and a brain," Holmes said without any modesty. "The portrait of the Colonel which hangs in his home showed a clear resemblance between him and his manservant. My suspicions were aroused as soon as I saw it."

"It's true," Mathews said. "I am the Colonel's son."

"One of the Colonel's two children?" I asked. "I thought that they were out of the city."

"They are," Holmes replied. "You see it took a little bit of digging – and not an inconsiderable amount of deductive reasoning – to discover that the Colonel had a child out of wedlock around the same time as the birth of his first child."

"It's true, Mr. Holmes," Mathews murmured. "According to my mother – a working class woman who has since died – the Colonel swept her off her feet. She fell madly in love with the blackguard and they had a child – me. Shortly after my birth, Colonel Cunningham announced to my mother that he was expecting another son…this time to the woman he had rightfully married. My mother was heartbroken and…she threw herself into the river late one evening. I was only a boy, but she instilled in me a hatred of that man, Mr. Holmes.

"The Colonel did his utmost to keep my existence a secret, but I would have none of it. When I came of age I insisted that I serve under him in the Boer War, lest I tell not only his family but the British public at large. What would the staunch, society-climbing Britons think of their great military hero then? The Colonel cared only for his reputation and, seeing that it was his only course of action, took me on as his batman. I served with him throughout the war and, when the conflict came to an end, I continued the blackmail. I hadn't much formal schooling so I knew that I needed some form of work. With the threat of public degradation hanging over him like a perpetual black cloud, I forced the Colonel to take me on as his manservant."

"Every time he opens his mouth you sound as if he's incriminating himself," Lestrade said. "Mr. Holmes, how can you be so certain that Mathews isn't the murderer?"

"My theory does, at present, stand upon conjecture, inspector," Holmes said. "However, I am quite sure that Mathews is innocent of the murder and – with any luck – I shall be able to substantiate my case very soon."

"But that doesn't explain why Mathews ran when we got on his scent," Lestrade said.

"With the overwhelming case against him, it's obvious that you'd suspect him of the murder. Not wishing to end up where he presently sits, Mathews fled."

From his waistcoat pocket, Holmes extracted his watch. "Oh, it is later than I had judged it to be, gentlemen and, with luck, I shall have an appointment at Baker Street which shall shed some much-needed light on this case. Come Watson!"

Holmes slipped out of the room and I followed wordlessly. We were soon ensconced in the belly of a hansom headed back for Baker Street. As was usual, Holmes remained silent about his plans. As our cab drew up outside of our lodgings, I saw my friend cast a gaze towards the windows above. His face a mask of uncertainty, Holmes entered the building and was greeted in the foyer by Mrs. Hudson.

"Ah, Mr. Holmes," she said to us both, "one of those street urchins came in here about fifteen minutes ago, pulling at the sleeve of another gentleman."

"One of the Irregulars! Excellent!"

Holmes bounded up the stairs and, following, I was stepping into our sitting room as Holmes wrung our visitor by the hand. He was a scruffy-looking man clutching a battered bowler hat in his hands. His scraggly auburn hair culminated in a pair of thick muttonchops on either side of his ruddy face.

"I got him, Mr. Holmes," beamed Wiggins, the head of Holmes's Baker Street Boys.

"Excellent work as usual, Wiggins," Holmes said. Turning to the man, Holmes gestured for him to take a seat. "I find it much easier to work with someone once I know his name."

"My name's Ryder," the man said, "Paul Ryder. Now see, here…this boy told me that there'd be a sovereign in this for me and —"

"You needn't fear, Mr. Ryder. You shall be compensated for your time here. Now then, answer for me a few questions. You're a cabbie, are you not?"

"I am, sir. Been employed in the city for five years."

"And on Friday last, were you instructed to wait outside a vacant house at number 12 Taviton Street?"

"I couldn't say whether it was a vacant house or not, sir."

"Of course not. But, you surely can tell me whether you aided someone in removing a corpse from that house, stowed it inside your hansom and then drove clear across the city and deposited the body inside an opium den."

"Now see here –"

The man rose and Holmes all but shoved him back into his seat. "I simply require a simple 'yes' or 'no' answer to my question. I can swear to it Mr. Ryder that you shall be implicated in complicity to murder if you do not cooperate."

Ryder sank back onto the sofa and stared at a spot between Holmes's shoes. "I did do as you say I did," he said at length. "I was told to keep quiet about the whole thing and if I did I'd be handsomely compensated for my work."

"Of course you would be," Holmes retorted.

He extracted a sovereign from his inner pocket and pressed it into the cabbie's hand. "Now that you have cleared your conscious Ryder, you can go even further and answer me one thing more: the person who instructed you to do this, can you describe him?"

"He was a nondescript fella," Ryder said. "He had a pale face, full lips and – though he kept his hat on all the time I saw him – he had dark hair. He was also a petite man. Thin he was. Almost like a lady."

Holmes eased the cabbie out of his seat. "Thank you, Mr. Ryder, you have been invaluable and – rest assured – I shall not speak one word of your involvement in this matter to anyone."

Once Holmes had sent Ryder and Wiggins away (the boy richer with a few coins as well), he eased into his chair and let out a satisfied sigh.

"Well?" I asked.

"I've solved it, Watson."

"Good God, Holmes," I said. "Please, keep me in suspense no longer and tell me what's going on. I confess that I'm very much in the dark."

"The pieces of the puzzle are simple ones to put together," he replied. "Alas, I cannot at the moment divulge the story in its entirety. However, first thing tomorrow morning I shall send off a cable and we will meet Lestrade at Colonel Cunningham's house. There, I shall endeavor to assemble those pieces of the puzzle as best as I can for you and the inspector."

I rose early the following morning and, though my wife was due back from the country, I hastily scrawled a note explaining my absence and rushed off to Baker Street to meet Holmes. I arrived in time to find Holmes spreading marmalade on a piece of toast as he partook of his breakfast. We ate in silence and, following his repast, I joined Holmes as he hailed a cab and gave our cabbie directions to the Colonel's house.

We found a police wagon had drawn up outside and Lestrade stood next to the vehicle a hand clasped on Mathews' shoulder.

"I don't know how you do it, Mr. Holmes," the inspector said as our odd group made it way to the door.

"On the whole this case was a rather simple one," my friend replied as he rang the bell. "For all of the murderer's attempts to disguise the thing, it was fairly easy to unravel."

The door was answered by Mrs. Cunningham and I daresay I saw a look of surprise cross her face as she came face-to-face with her butler who was still manacled and in the custody of an arm of the law. She nevertheless showed us inside and graciously relieved us of our hats and coats. Holmes then made his way into the formal sitting room and instructed for us all to take seats.

"Now," he began standing in the middle of the room, his long arms clasped behind his back, "I find it best to present the facts in the case of the death of Colonel Walter Cunningham to you in this way: in the order to which they were presented to me. On Friday evening, my friend and colleague, Dr. John Watson, and I were approached by a woman named Mrs. Louisa McGinty, a resident of Birmingham and a stranger to the city of London. Arriving with the intent of visiting her children, she was making her way to Piccadilly Circus when she happened to get lost and stumbled upon a scene of singular grotesqueness. Watching from afar, she saw two men carry the body of a third out of a house and into a hansom cab which then trundled off into the night.

"Beginning the investigation, I knew that the key to solving the case would be to identify the dead man. In all probability, whoever was responsible for his murder would be associated with him in some way which would give me suspects among whom I could begin searching for the killer. I landed upon Colonel Cunningham as the most probable candidate. Having disappeared the night before Mrs. McGinty witnessed what she did, it seemed very likely that the case of the Colonel's disappearance the murder she witnessed were connected. Investigating here for clues, I came upon a small box which was stowed in the Colonel's desk – a desk which contained a hypodermic syringe and a bottle of cocaine. Even more curious was the note which I found in the Colonel's desk which simply had the address 12 Taviton Street written upon it.

"Figuring that Taviton Street was the most likely scene of the crime – and the street on which Mrs. McGinty found herself on Friday evening, I found the piece which joined the two cases together. The last piece of the puzzle which I needed to sort out was the cabbie. Per Mrs. McGinty's story, one of the men who was assisting with the carrying of the body scrambled to the top of the hansom and drove off. A cabbie was therefore imperative in the murderer's scheme for he would be the perfect person to expertly weave a hansom conveying a dead man across the city to its final destination.

"So, as it stands, Colonel Cunningham returned home from his club on Thursday evening, went into his study with the intent of using the drugs which were hidden in his desk. However, his rendezvous at number 12 Taviton Street was more important to the Colonel at the time, he left, arrived at the address given to him where he was murdered in the vacant house and then carted across town by his murderer and the cabbie. This scenario produces two curious questions namely: why did the Colonel suddenly change his mind and leave his study if his drug habit was so intense, and why should the murderer risk exposure by placing the Colonel's body inside a hansom cab when he could just as easily have left it inside the vacant house at number 12?

"To answer one of these questions, I defer to Inspector Lestrade of Scotland Yard. Inspector, when you looked the body over at the morgue, did you see any signs of drug use – perhaps more specifically intravenous drug use of the sort which might be suggested by the Colonel having in his possession a bottle of cocaine and a syringe?"

"No, Mr. Holmes," Lestrade replied. "I checked myself and that fact can be verified by the coroner."

"I am not entirely unfamiliar with drug use of that sort," Holmes said and I swore I detected a waver in his tone, "and users of the drug are marked by marks on their arms – the most common point of injection. So, I came to the conjecture that Colonel Cunningham was not a drug user at all. The box which was in his desk and the opium den in which he was discovered were simply used to throw us off the scent and, I believe, to do something far worse. You see, with the news of his supposed drug habit becoming public, the Colonel's reputation would be tarnished forever. Whoever murdered the Colonel wished to ruin him – even after death.

"This does point the finger of suspicion at Mathews, the butler. We have, of course, since learned that Mathews was the Colonel's illegitimate son who confessed quite openly that he would have gladly bruised the status of the man who drove his mother to suicide. However, Mathews was indebted to the man he hated so. The Colonel took Mathews on as his military batman and then opened up his home to him. Needless to say, the Colonel did this to save himself from scandal, but Mathews had a means of living. Should he kill the Colonel – even if he did receive a portion of the Colonel's wealth – he would be forced to find employment elsewhere. Therefore, I ruled out Mathews. That left only one person who could have any reason to murder Colonel Cunningham."

Holmes turned to face Mrs. Cunningham, his dark grey eyes boring into her being with the intensity of a wild conflagration.

"Mr. Holmes," the woman said, "you must be joking."

"I very much wish that this were a jest, Mrs. Cunningham," Holmes said, "however the evidence against you is quite strong. It may not, perhaps, convince a judge and jury but, for the moment, I think that I can win over the officer of the law who is present in this room.

"You see, Mrs. Cunningham, I am certain that you saw a resemblance between your Colonel and Mathews. You were hurt. The Colonel had had a child out of wedlock and had instituted that child into your home. His lying was the turning point for you. I daresay that the rumors which circulated suggesting that you were only interested in the Colonel's wealth may be rooted in truth and, though I am loath to theorize on the precise nature of your sinister machinations, perhaps you found this decades-old infidelity some justification for exacting your wicked scheme. You were then willing to do anything to get at the man's money and you concocted a plot to murder him and then claim his inheritance.

"You were conveniently upstairs, away from your husband when he returned home on Thursday evening. The note which you had written was on his desk and, though he may have recognized your handwriting, he did not go to confront you. Instead he left, playing into your hands at once. You then left, perhaps leaving by a second exit so as to not elicit suspicion from Mathews downstairs. Along the way you met with your unwilling compatriot, Paul Ryder, a cabbie. It was while you were riding in his cabbie that you changed into a second set of clothes.

"I confess, Mrs. Cunningham that you did have me fooled for some time with that simple disguise. I have fallen for the ploy before but it was with utmost sincerity that Mrs. Louisa McGinty told us of the two men who carried the body into the hansom cab that I believed her. However, when I visited Taviton Street for myself I became aware of the fact that the street has very few streetlamps. In the darkness and wearing a set of men's clothes, it is quiet understandable how Mrs. McGinty may have mistaken you for one of the male sex. My suspicions were confirmed when I remembered that you were an actress who would have no doubt been quite used to wearing men's clothing and when Mr. Ryder visited my rooms last evening he described a petite, almost feminine man as the mastermind of the scheme.

"To ruin your late husband, you dumped the body unceremoniously inside the opium den. The proprietor of that shop is an acquaintance of mine and he confessed to being won over by the money which you offered him to turn a blind eye while you deposited the Colonel's body within the den. Then, returning home you entered the way you had left rid yourself of the garb which you had adopted and then stole down into the Colonel's study where you placed that box with the syringe and bottle in his desk. Though the box was kept in the bottommost drawer of the desk, it was hardly hidden. A man like the Colonel should certainly wish to keep his vice as inconspicuous as possible and leaving it out *atop* the other papers in that drawer was noticeable in the extreme. What's more the case was clean and neat as though it were new. The Colonel could hardly have been the regular drug user which you wished to portray him as if the box were new."

Sherlock Holmes concluded his oration. He moved away from the center of the room, withdrew his cigarette case from his inner pocket and lit a cigarette.

"You are correct," Mrs. Cunningham said at length. "You are correct on all counts. I have no need to hide from the truth and, though I am sure that you are about to tell me that anything I have to say may be used in evidence against me, Inspector, I have no need to fear the hangman's rope. I acted my part rather well, wouldn't you say? If I fooled the great Sherlock Holmes – even for an instant – then I should say that I played my part well."

Mrs. Cunningham was escorted out of the house by Lestrade whom I have never seen look quite so crestfallen and on edge in my life. Finishing his cigarette, Holmes tossed it into the empty hearth and moved into the foyer to collect our hats and coats.

"Well, Mathews," he said turning to the butler who had come to help us with our garments, "I think you shall have a sizeable fortune coming to you now."

As I eased my sleeve into my coat Mathews stared Holmes squarely in the eye.

"I don't want it, Mr. Holmes," he said. "Colonel Cunningham did nothing for me and I have only stayed with him out of sheer necessity. Now that he is gone I shall endeavor to find work elsewhere. I believe that I have come to be quite a good butler and with any luck I shall be welcomed by some of this city's nobility."

"I think that you shall, Mathews," Holmes replied. "If employment as a butler does not suit you, might I suggest a life as a bareknuckle boxer? Seldom have I seen an uppercut executed so beautifully in my life."

Holmes flashed a grin exposing his false canine. I swore that I saw the ghost of a smile cross Mathews' face.

"Well now, Watson," said Holmes clasping me on the shoulder, "I am sure that you wish to return to that wife of yours, however could I possibly persuade you to accompany me to luncheon and from there to Piccadilly Circus? I rather think that Mrs. Louisa McGinty deserves to hear this tale told."

The Haunting of
Hamilton Gardens

"Good God," I said as I returned my cup of coffee to the saucer, nearly losing a large quantity of my drink. I stared at the morning newspaper in my hand and tried to make sense of the headline. No matter how fast the cogs in my brain worked however, I remained just as surprised as when I had first come across it.

I see that I have once more fallen into the pattern of telling these tales wrong end foremost. To begin, it was a cool, autumn morning in 1897. I had been away from Baker Street – and London for that matter – having spent two weeks in the country in the company of an old friend from the Fifth Northumberland Fusiliers. It had been a gratifying two weeks, though at the end of the time which was spent in much reminiscing and relaxing out-of-doors, I found myself exhausted. I had fallen asleep on the train back to the city and, arriving at Baker Street late, I ascended the steps to my room in silence. I could see light emanating from the door to the sitting room and knew that Holmes was still up; no doubt lost in thought, wreathed in a fog of thick pipe smoke. However, being far too tired to announce my presence, I went up to my room and virtually collapsed upon the bed.

I managed to rouse myself early the following morning and after I had set about putting away my things, I shaved and dressed and made my way downstairs for breakfast. Sherlock Holmes had already risen and dressed and was languidly flipping through the morning edition of *The Times* when I entered the sitting room. My friend greeted me warmly and said that there was much to discuss, though, he told me, he would wait until after I had broken my fast to begin his oration. I sat down at the breakfast table, poured a cup of coffee, and unfolded the copy of *The Star* and promptly let out the exclamation of surprise.

"You have seen the paper then?" Holmes asked.

"Yes," I stammered. "Holmes, what does it mean?"

I returned my gaze to the sheet of newsprint and the large headline which had grabbed my attention. It ran:

Sherlock Holmes Wages War on Prominent Spiritualist

"If you read the article I daresay that you shall learn very quickly what it means," Holmes coldly replied. "What's more, the reporter for *The Star* might be able to relay facts to you more concisely than I ever could."

I regarded the newspaper in my hand with some contention. I was not a frequent reader of *The Star* for I found it to be overly lurid and in poor taste. I could still recall that during the autumn of 1888 during the horrible Jack the Ripper murders, it was *The Star* which carried the most sensational details of the case, sparing little thought for the public at large or for the kith and kin of the murderer's victims. I shall not mention that foul business further for our involvement in that matter is one which I am afraid I can never make public.

In hindsight, I should have found its presence on the breakfast table curious in the extreme, but I suppose Holmes had gotten a copy for his own amusement. I looked at the writer's name.

"'Mr. William Parker,'" I read aloud.

"An amiable young man in his own way," Holmes said. "Oh, come now, Watson. Do not regard that piece of pulp with such derision. Allow me ten minutes more and you shall hear the business through to the end. I cabled Mr. Parker this morning after I rose and requested that he come 'round to Baker Street to relay the whole situation to you."

"You asked him to come around just for my benefit?" I asked, rather touched.

"And for mine too," Holmes added. "It can never hurt to hear the details of a case again. I very nearly have the thing solved, however my solution lacks evidence. And evidence is the one thing I need if I am to win over Sir Jeffrey Curbishly."

"I take it then that this Sir Jeffrey is the prominent spiritualist?"

"Precisely," Holmes said. "Sir Jeffrey – and a great deal of London – has also reached a conclusion to this whole, nasty business. However, his culprit is rather difficult to go and clap irons on I'm afraid."

"Oh? Why's that?"

"Because, my dear Watson," Holmes said, "Sir Jeffrey points the finger of suspicion firmly at the devil himself."

I confess that a faint chill ran up my spine at these words. A moment later, the bell chimed below. Holmes extracted his watch from his waistcoat. "Excellent," he said noting the time, "Parker's five minutes earlier than expected."

My friend rushed out of the room and left me in stupefied silence until he returned a moment later with a young man following behind. He could not have been more than six-and-twenty and his young face bespoke of some naïveté; it was obvious that the young man was not as world-weary as Holmes or I. He was well-dressed, and carried a bowler hat in his long, dexterous-looking fingers.

"Mr. William Parker," Holmes began by way of introduction, "allow me to introduce you to my friend and colleague, Dr. John Watson."

"A pleasure to meet you, Doctor," Parker said. "I have read all your accounts of Mr. Holmes's work."

"Thank you," said I.

Holmes gestured for our guest to sit. "You will forgive the good doctor for a few moments while he breaks his fast. It would be remiss of me should I not allow him to enjoy a hearty meal on the day after his return from the country. All the same, I should like you to go over the details of this case – for both the doctor's benefit and my own."

Parker settled back in his chair. From his inner breast pocket, he withdrew a small, black notebook which he opened. "Well, I suppose I ought to begin with a few particulars about myself. I am a reporter for *The Star* and I have been in my present situation for nearly four years. In that time, I have reported on dozens of stories of all varieties. Some of us at *The Star* have a bit of a specialty; I am afraid that I have yet to find mine. While I may be young (and not as experienced as some of the other writers on the paper), I like to think my skills set me apart from the others. I am something of a favorite of Mr. Parke, the editor, as well.

"This current matter was brought to my attention two weeks prior by an associate of mine who lives in the region of St John's Wood. It was he who brought me to the attention of Mrs. Emily Cardew and her daughter, Lillian, who currently reside at number 41 Hamilton Gardens.

"Some description of the neighborhood might be in order for you to accurately perceive what section of the city we are dealing with. As one can imagine, the area is quite nice; surely one of the more upper-class sections of London. The homes which make up Hamilton Gardens are part of Alma Square and they are small, two-story affairs which stand in rows one beside the next. I feel as if this is an important fact as skeptics – such as Mr. Holmes – could make the claim that the family is trying to move into a more salubrious section of the city. However, as they already reside in one of the most fashionable districts of London, that claim *does* seem to be easily refuted.

"Onto the principal people in the case." Parker turned over a page in his notebook as I settled into my chair and reached for my own. "The woman is Mrs. Emily Cardew, formerly Miss Emily Melville. She is thirty-six years of age and has lived at 41 Hamilton Gardens with her daughter for three years. Her daughter, Lillian, is eleven. Mrs. Cardew was of good social standing - her father having held a minor position in Her Majesty's government. That same year she wed a young officer – Lieutenant Cardew – who, the following year, was killed in the Mahdist War just before the birth of his child."

"The name is familiar to me," I said as I took it down. "Having served in the Afghan campaign, I have tried to stay abreast of my fellow military officers."

"The lieutenant was a decorated officer, doctor. Anyway, Mrs. Cardew lived off of her late father's money as well as that of her late husband. She was also supported financially by the lieutenant's family to whom she had grown quite close. They helped her raise her child and school her. Through it all, Mrs. Cardew never seemed intent on marrying again, though she had gained something of a reputation in society. And, for what it is worth, I found Mrs. Cardew to be a very handsome woman on the occasions when I spoke with her.

"Now, as I mentioned, Mrs. Cardew and her daughter moved into 41 Hamilton Gardens three years ago and by all accounts their time there was happy and quiet. Neighbors – including my associate – said that they kept much to themselves, but they were always very friendly in passing. On occasion, some of the other school children in the neighborhood would go to play at the Cardews, or Lillian was invited to play at another's house. Their quiet routine was not altered until two weeks ago.

"According to Mrs. Cardew, in the early hours of the morning of 3 October, she thought that she heard the sound of someone moving about in the house. At first, she thought it was nothing. However, when she heard it again a few moments later – this time even more loudly than before – she sat up and lit a lamp. The sound grew nearer and a moment later she saw its source: her daughter, Lillian, was walking in her sleep. Lillian entered her mother's room and stood in the doorway, appearing almost to sway to and fro, before she turned and went back the way she had come."

"Did Lillian routinely suffer from somnambulism?" I asked.

"According to her mother, never," Parker replied. "And, I am afraid that that fact makes what follows all the more distressing. According to Mrs. Cardew, the following day Lillian had no memory whatsoever of the incident, despite her mother's many efforts to question her daughter about it. Lillian, according to her mother, was fine for the remainder of the day and even went to play with one of the little girls who live in the neighborhood."

"Did that little girl's mother have anything to say about Lillian Cardew?" Holmes asked.

"When questioned about it, she said that there appeared to be nothing wrong with Lillian whatsoever. However, once more, in the early hours of the following morning, Lillian Cardew rose from her bed and began to walk in her sleep. However, this time Mrs. Cardew insists that she could hear her daughter muttering something under her breath. Later, when she questioned her daughter, Mrs. Cardew discovered that Lillian had no memory of having woken in the night, but there were dark circles under her eyes which she attributed to the lack of sleep which came with two consecutive nights of sleepwalking.

"So, in order to get to the root of the problem, Mrs. Cardew endeavored to sit outside her daughter's room. In the event that her daughter was roused from her sleep once more, she would be on hand to tuck her in. Mrs. Cardew says that once again in the early hours of the morning, she was roused from sleep (having drifted off herself) and found that her daughter had sat upright in bed and was murmuring once more under her breath. Mrs. Cardew lighted a lamp and drew closer to Lillian's bed and discovered, quite to her horror that Lillian's eyes appeared to have rolled back in her head. The whites of her eyes shone brightly in the guttering flame of the lamp."

"And what was young Lillian Cardew muttering about?" Holmes asked.

William Parker adjusted his tie nervously. "She was speaking some sort of nonsense about the house being her own and that she and her mother would have to leave immediately. She repeated that phrase over and over again: 'This house is mine. This house is mine.'"

I looked to Holmes however his face was cold and unreadable. He had closed his eyes – absorbing this information once more – but whether he found the story credible or not, I could not say. I have always been a rational man, but this new development suddenly put Holmes's cryptic statement about the devil in a whole new light. I confess that for an instant I knew not what to think and I reached for my cigarette case to steady my nerves.

Without opening his eyes, Holmes said: "I trust, Mr. Parker that you shall not object to Dr. Watson lighting a cigarette? I confess that I am rather craving my first pipe of the morning."

"By all means, gentlemen."

Holmes reached for his pipe and began to fill it with tobacco from the Persian slipper on the mantelpiece. "Speaking objectively," said he, "I can understand where the rumors of *demonic possession* are originating. However, you know as well as I that the facts in this case are very much in their infancy. Please continue, Mr. Parker."

Holmes struck a match and lighted his pipe as Parker continued. "Well," he said, "Mrs. Cardew decided that the next course of action would be to speak with a doctor. A medical man was brought to the house – one Dr. Douglas Flaugherty - and he conducted an examination of Lillian Cardew. I have interviewed the doctor on two occasions and both times he told me outright that there was nothing at all wrong with the girl."

Holmes suddenly stood from his chair and moved to his desk where he rifled through a pile of papers. He extracted from the stack a folded-up copy of *The Star* and read aloud: "Your own words, Mr. Parker: 'Dr. Flaugherty says that Lillian Cardew's pulse and breathing were normal. There appeared to be no sign of any illness, and even an inspection of the girl's eyes – which often yields up unseen evidence from the brain – could conclude nothing.'"

"Precisely, Mr. Holmes," Parker said, "but Lillian's condition did not get any better. In fact, it only got worse. Following the doctor's examination, Mrs. Cardew believed that, perhaps, her daughter was suffering from a mental disorder. Over the course of a few days she corresponded with a physician on Wimpole Street who is a follower of the psychoanalytic theory which is being pioneered by Dr. Freud. Mrs. Cardew was prepared to take Lillian in for a consultation, when, once more in the dead of night, Lillian had another outburst. This was one was far more violent in nature and she appeared to be gyrating madly on her bed. She thrashed about in her sheets and uttered oaths of the most deplorable nature. Gnashing her teeth and snarling, she continued to repeat: 'This house is mine.'"

"And," said Holmes, "there was a witness."

"Yes," Parker replied. "Mrs. Ellen Mortimer. She is a friend of Mrs. Cardew's and was, in fact, the mother of the girl whom Lillian went to play with only days before. Mrs. Mortimer had already said that she could see nothing wrong with Lillian Cardew but, having seen how frightened her mother was getting over the whole business, Mrs. Mortimer insisted on spending the evening with the Cardews."

"And this Mrs. Mortimer witnessed the violent outbursts of which you spoke?" I asked.

By way of an answer, Holmes quoted from the same article: "'I watched in horror,' said Mrs. Mortimer, 'as little Lillian Cardew convulsed wildly on her bed. It was as though she was a puppet being conducted by some great, invisible hand pulling at strings from above. All the while – as she convulsed, twisted, and knotted herself up on her bed – she said things, truly horrible things, in a voice which I swear could not have come from the girl I have known so well. I knew in that moment that this was no longer an earthly matter. This little girl had become possessed by some malignant, evil power whose might I dare not attempt to contemplate.' All rather lurid stuff."

"The morning after this display, Mrs. Mortimer implored Mrs. Cardew to seek out the services of a priest."

I sat for a moment in stunned silence. "A priest?" I said at length. "To perform an exorcism?"

"Quite right, Dr. Watson," Parker replied. "As the matter stands, no such action has occurred leaving this story without an ending. It is for that reason that so many newspapers have been scrambling to fill in the details of the story thus far."

"And in doing so," said Sherlock Holmes as he returned to his seat, "your newspaper – as well as the other papers which have covered this incident – have created something of a sensation in

London. There are few in all circles of society who have not spoken of the curious haunting of Hamilton Gardens."

"It is remarkable," I said at length. "It is simply too fantastic to contemplate."

"Tell me, Parker," Holmes said, "in your interview with Mrs. Mortimer, how did she strike you?"

"She is a quiet, reserved woman," Parker said. He opened his notebook and consulted his notes. "She is forty years of age – four years Mrs. Cardew's senior – and has been married to her husband for fifteen years. They have two children: the first is the same age as Lillian Cardew and the other two years younger. I found her to be a very amiable woman."

"Did it strike you as an out-of-character act for Mrs. Mortimer to suggest seeking the aid of a priest to perform an exorcism?"

"No. In my interview with her, Mrs. Mortimer described herself as 'religious and God-fearing.' It is, I suppose, somewhat natural than for her to seek a theological explanation for this turn of events."

Holmes once more withdrew his watch from his waistcoat pocket. "My, how the times does fly, Mr. Parker. I shan't keep you longer; however there are one or two things which I think would be invaluable to me. First and foremost, are there any photographs of Mrs. Cardew and her daughter?"

"For the sake of her daughter, Mrs. Cardew refused to allow our photographer to take pictures."

"That is most unfortunate. I would find them most illuminating," Holmes said. "Secondly, what church did Mrs. Ellen Mortimer regularly attend?"

After Parker had supplied the name and address of the church, he excused himself from our room. Holmes closed the door behind him and, as soon as he had eased it shut, he let out a loud burst of laughter.

"Forgive me, Watson," he said as he crossed back to his chair. He eased back and crossed one long leg over the other. "My laughter is ill-advised for we do tread in dark territory I'm afraid."

"You aren't seriously suggesting that the poor girl has become possessed by some demon, are you?"

"I should hope that you know me well enough, Watson, that I refute that explanation wholeheartedly. No, despite what the majority of London's populace may believe – and what the ignorant Sir Jeffrey Curbishly insists on proliferating – this is a simple matter of deception."

"By Mrs. Cardew?"

"Yes," Holmes replied languidly. "And she has involved her daughter in the scheme as well. I am certain of it."

"But what motive should they have for doing such a thing?"

"That is one of the few pieces of the puzzle which I have been unable to put into place. Until I can do so, I am afraid that my rational explanation shall be ignored."

"When were you first consulted on the matter?" I asked.

"Only days ago," Holmes answered. "I confess that I had not been following the case, being preoccupied with far more important matters. However, when Parker turned up on my doorstep asking for my opinion I could not help but become involved in the business. Apparently after finding a cogent explanation for the Baskerville business, I have gained something of a reputation in certain circles as a debunker of ghosts."

Holmes spoke in a tone which did not mask his evident derision. Filling his pipe once more, I was about to do the same when we were arrested by the sound of the bell ringing below. A moment later, Mrs. Hudson entered with the card of our visitor. Passing it to Holmes, he glanced at it before smirking mischievously and handing it off to me.

The name of our guest: Sir Jeffrey Curbishly.

The man who entered our sitting room moments later was tall and broad-shouldered, carrying in a gloved hand a silk top hat and wrapped in an expensive-looking greatcoat done over with a fur collar. He appeared to be in his mid-forties for his temples had begun to grey giving him an air of authority which complimented his learned-looking countenance. As he stepped into the room, I watched his dark eyes meet Holmes's. My friend arched an eyebrow ever so slightly and then wordlessly gestured for our visitor to take a seat on the settee.

Curbishly silently crossed the room and took a seat, his eye still trained on Holmes with peculiar intensity.

"Ah, Sir Jeffrey," Holmes said, feigning a cordial tone as he struck a match and lighted his pipe, "I do not think that you have had the pleasure of meeting my friend and colleague, Dr. John Watson."

"I have not," Curbishly replied. "It is a pleasure, Doctor. I have read your accounts of Mr. Holmes's work with keen interest."

"Now then," said Holmes as he settled back in his chair, crossing one leg over the other in a deceptively languid manner, "what brings you to my home?"

"You know very well what brings me here." From his inner breast pocket, Curbishly withdrew a folded-up copy of *The Star*; the same one which still sat on our breakfast table. "This article."

"You must not blame me for the rather cavalier use of the phrase *wages war*. I usually hold the journalistic profession in some esteem; however, I do believe that the amiable Mr. Parker did overstep his boundaries at his typewriter."

"This is not a simple matter of semantics," Curbishly retorted. "This is a blatant attempt to tarnish my image."

"I never did desire to do anything of the kind," Holmes replied. "In fact, Sir Jeffrey, I do hold your *scientific* work in high regard. I could not think of a more suited figure to be knighted for such contributions to the field as you. However, since you have begun spouting this spiritualist claptrap, I cannot help but consider you a particularly nasty impediment to solving this case. That is – as you should know – my sole desire in the matter."

It was Curbishly's turn to smirk now. "Ah, you cannot admit when you are wrong. You cannot help but fight back when you've been bested. You should know as well as I that this business is firmly rooted in the supernatural."

"I do not see what leads you to such an assessment," Holmes retorted. "All of the evidence which has been made public to me suggests a rational explanation."

"Then perhaps you would care to explain the Ouija board…and the other reported supernatural phenomenon which are connected to 41 Hamilton Gardens?"

"Pardon me," I said, "but what do you mean when you refer to the Ouija board?"

Curbishly smirked again. "Have you been withholding evidence from the good doctor in order to further your case?"

Holmes rolled his eyes.

"Allow me to elucidate, Doctor. Perhaps you may not have known, but I was one of the first people who was involved in this business after it took the public's attention. I have for some time been something of a public figure after I began a serious study of spiritualism. What started out as a passing interest in the subject – certainly you cannot deny asking yourself what happens after death – soon became a passion of mine. In my studies, I came to learn more about the spirit world. But, I have also come to learn about a host of other entities which exist outside our own world. It is one of these entities that is responsible for the haunting of Hamilton Gardens.

"Imagine if you will, Dr. Watson, a soap bubble floating in the air. It – for the purpose of this explanation – represents the world in which we live. It is composed of all the settled orders of nature and laws of science which I have held dear in my line of work and which you, no doubt, also studied greatly before becoming a doctor. However, I ask you, Doctor: how likely is one to find a single, isolated soap bubble floating in the air? It seldom occurs. There are other soap bubbles which float and bounce around alongside of it. And these other bubbles represent their own worlds. However, they do not operate in the same manner as our world does. Some of these worlds are merely worlds of ideas and concepts, filled with intangible notions. Others are far more perceptible. They are the worlds inhabited by those who have shuffled off this mortal coil.

"The other difference between the real world and the analogy which I have just presented to you is that it is impossible for two soap bubbles to interact with one another. Should the two collide, they would burst. However, picture if you will, Dr. Watson, the bubble which represents our world attaching itself to one of these other bubbles. A clear link between the two has been forged."

I cast a glance in Holmes's direction and found my friend with his eyes closed, pulling on his pipe. His brow was knitted with a look of derision. Holmes -- ever the skeptic, ever the rationalist, who believed only in what could be calculated, observed, and studied --

could not help but find Curbishly's talk impossible to digest. I tried not to mirror my friend's contempt towards the spiritualist. I thought that there could be something to be gained from his words which might stimulate something in Holmes and lead him to a conclusion.

"There are many methods in bridging the gap between our world and another," Curbishly continued. "Perhaps the most common sort is the séance. I perceive that you are familiar with the practice, doctor?"

"I am," I replied. In our time together, Holmes and I had been called in to investigate spiritualists who would con the public out of their money with cheap trick shows and conjuring tricks at such séances.

"However, the method which figures directly in the case of Lillian Cardew is the aforementioned Ouija board -- a device which is used to contact spirits from another world. The person using the board is guided by the hand of a spirit and may communicate with them in this manner. I have seen a number of successful demonstrations of the Ouija board in my time, however these devices do present a hazard for the user and I believe that young Lillian Cardew fell victim to a spirit after using an Ouija board.

"As I mentioned already, Doctor, I was one of the first people to be involved in the Hamilton Gardens case. I met with Mrs. Cardew and observed her daughter from afar. When I visited the household, I could see young Lillian Cardew laying in her bed in a terribly weakened state, still groaning and muttering under her breath in a voice which I am certain was not her own. With her mother's consent, I was able to search through a few of the girl's possessions and came across a Ouija board. It was a crude, make-shift type, but spirits are not particular. Mrs. Cardew insisted that she had never seen it before. However, I was certain now that the board had to be connected to Lillian's strange behavior and I endeavored to find out when she had used it. I spoke to a number of the children who reside in the neighborhood. One of them told me of how she and Lillian had been playing with the board one day.

"Armed with this knowledge, I began to investigate the house itself: number 41 Hamilton Gardens. Before Mrs. Cardew moved into the residence three years ago, it was occupied by the Wheelwrights – Horace and Patricia. According to my research – which I can easily verify should you desire it – Patricia Wheelwright died eight years ago. Her husband died two years later. You may ask what connection this has with the rest of the case. I shall tell you: according to the child with whom Lillian Cardew played with the Ouija board, the spirit who they managed to contact was named *Horace*."

"And you believe that the ghost of Horace Wheelwright is responsible for the strange goings-on now?"

"Not quite, Dr. Watson." Curbishly leaned forward in his seat. "You see – to return to my soap bubble analogy – just as one bubble can connect to another, imagine a number of soap bubbles connected like the links of a chain. In this way, an entity from one world could travel through various worlds and into our own. This is undoubtedly frightening for, as I have been quite vocal pointing out, I believe that the devil – or one of his agents – is responsible for possessing and corrupting Lillian Cardew."

Sherlock Holmes snorted loudly.

"Just as the spirit of Horace Wheelwright made it into our world," Curbishly continued unabashed, "I believe that a demon used the poor man's spirit as a means of free transport. Unwittingly, Lillian Cardew was corrupted by the demon as she used the Ouija board to communicate with the spirit world."

"What evidence do you have to support this claim?" I asked.

"There can be no other explanation," Curbishly replied with steadfast resolve. "I have read the witness testimony and I can assure you that there is no possible way for a young girl to contort herself and writhe as she did under her own power. It is simply a physical impossibility."

Sir Jeffrey Curbishly sat back on the settee with a smug expression etched on his face. "Well," he said at length, "what do you have to say to that, Mr. Holmes?"

For what masqueraded as an eternity, Sherlock Holmes sat calmly pulling on his pipe. At length, he laid it aside, sat back in his chair and pressed the tips of his fingers together in his usual gesture of contemplation. "I do not believe a word of what you have to say," he quietly said. "You have put forth no evidence to support your claim and in my line of work cold, hard evidence is an imperative component to solving any problem. Therefore, Sir Jeffrey, I shall not resolve to do anything about the newspaper headline to which you took such offense. If all-out war is what you desire, then I shall only be too happy to oblige."

"What are you saying, Holmes?"

"I am saying that I can present a logical explanation to the Hamilton Gardens case in twenty-four hours' time. And, what is more, I needn't even leave my rooms here at Baker Street to do it. I am in possession of nearly all the facts and, what I do not know off-handedly, I can ascertain with the help of Dr. Watson and my other agents. By the time that the last edition of *The Star* goes to press tomorrow evening, you shall find my explanation therein."

Another palpable silence descended over the sitting room, Sir Jeffrey Curbishly stared into space. I could read in his eyes a look of befuddlement. I could read the man well that he was the sort who always believed that he was in in total control of any situation, but for once in his life he seemed to know not where to turn. Curbishly drew in a deep breath and stood from his seat.

"Very well, Mr. Holmes," he said as he placed his hat back on his head, "if you wish to act in this manner then I shall not do anything to prevent you from making a fool of yourself. I fully expect you to be a man of your word."

"My word is my bond, Sir Jeffrey."

The ghost of a smirk flashed across Holmes's face and, wordlessly, Curbishly turned sharply on his heel and exited the room.

As soon as he had pulled the door shut behind him, Sherlock Holmes erupted in laughter.

"I hazard a guess that Sir Jeffrey felt rather the part of the fool," Holmes said. "Surely he came in here with the intent of winning me over to his point-of-view and if he succeeded not with me then certainly with you, my dear fellow. Have you ever heard someone deliver such drivel with such authority? Oh, Sir Jeffrey Curbishly would make a handsome sum for himself if he made his living in the prosperous con artist trade."

"But do you think that what you have done is wise, Holmes?" I asked. "I have never been one to question your powers, but certainly you have made your situation needlessly complex by imposing on yourself confinement to this place?"

"Hmm? Oh, I beg pardon, Watson; my mind was elsewhere. You need not worry about me." Holmes rubbed his hands together delightfully. "I shall relish this game between Curbishly and myself. And a game it shall be. If I know Sir Jeffrey as I think I do than he will doubtlessly take this rivalry deadly seriously and I would not be in the least bit surprised to find a man posted on the opposite side of the street to ensure the fact that I do not break my word and leave these premises."

"Then what do you intend to do if you are indeed going to be a veritable prisoner here for the next day?" I asked.

"I shall first send a telegram to the amiable Mr. Parker and tell him of this new development. This is the sort of stuff the press simply takes to like a fly to honey. And then, I shall see if Mrs. Hudson is willing to scare us up some luncheon. This case has already consumed our morning and now part of early afternoon. We shall no more speak of it."

Holmes was true to his word and refused to speak of the matter whilst we dined. In the meantime, he pressed me for information about my two weeks in the country and I was only too willing to share my reminiscences of the past fortnight.

Just after we had had our dishes cleared away, Billy, the pageboy, scampered up the seventeen steps to our rooms carrying the latest edition of *The Star*. Holmes zealously paged through it and let out an exclamation as he clapped eyes on the desired article.

"Ah, Parker has done his job up to snuff once more," Holmes said. The article read:

Sherlock Holmes Challenges Spiritualist to Game of Wits

According to the great detective, Mr. Sherlock Holmes himself, he is close to providing an explanation for the mysterious events which have transpired at number 41 Hamilton Gardens which have so enraptured the public. Holmes says that he refutes the assertions of noted spiritualist Sir Jeffrey Curbishly who has provided a supernatural explanation for the case. In order to prove Curbishly wrong, Holmes has promised to solve the case in twenty-four hours without leaving his rooms on Baker Street. This reporter shall carry the story as news develops and will print Holmes's explanation of the case when it is provided to him.

"That article will certainly incite Curbishly's temper," I said.

"Just what I hoped to do," Holmes remarked with a wry grin. "While Sir Jeffrey may have taken matters to an extreme when he accused me of wishing to tarnish his image, I confess that there is some latent bullying behind my actions. I do it not entirely for myself though, old friend. If Curbishly continues to proliferate his fantastic theories, then dozens of hapless and unsuspecting people will continue to believe in his words and fall right into the hands of the charlatans and tricksters we have spent time exposing. There is more at stake in this case than is readily apparent."

Holmes moved to his chair and took a seat, stretching his long frame out and once more pressing the tips of his fingers together.

"Well," I said at length, "you do not have much time. If this really is a game of wits between you and Curbishly, what is your first move?"

"I feel as though a visit to the scene is imperative," Holmes replied. "I confess that I have yet to venture forth to Hamilton Gardens, and seeing as it is impossible for me to do so now, I must ask for your help, my dear fellow."

"I shall only be too happy to help in any way that I can," I answered.

"Excellent," Holmes cried. "Then away you must to number 41 Hamilton Gardens. The place has become a center of attention in this city so there is some police activity there. I would not be surprised should you meet a constable or even good old Stanley Hopkins in the midst of your sojourn. But, make your way to the house and report back to me everything you see and hear. As Parker told us, the scene is a most unusual one for events of this kind to transpire. I shall ask you to perform one small, but utterly vital task for me: I shall need you to procure for me a picture of the two women concerned in this business. That should be the last link in the chain for me to build my case."

Silence fell over the room as Holmes then seemed to forget all about the events of the morning yet again and busied himself with his chemical apparatus. I, feeling as though I should wait for my friend's directive before going on my mission, settled in with a book and my pipe and whiled away much of the afternoon in a contemplative silence.

Mrs. Hudson brought us our dinner and we ate; Holmes most heartily which was most gratifying for me as I knew of Holmes's bad habits in foregoing sustenance when he was occupied with work. After our supper was cleared away, Holmes inspected his watch and drummed his fingers anxiously on the table. He lit a cigarette and cast a dark glance into the street below.

"The hour approaches when you should make your way to the scene," he murmured with a foreboding undertone in his voice.

I drew up to the window where Holmes stood and parted the curtain to cast a glance into the thoroughfare below. Just as Holmes had said earlier, there was a man standing on the opposite side of the street. He was dressed in a handsome but simple suit of clothes and appeared to be in the process of lighting a pipe. Holmes let out a bemused exclamation.

"Judging from the none-too-small pile of matches by his foot, I should say that our friend has been standing in that spot for at least two hours. Sir Jeffrey is certainly the competitive sort. I shouldn't wish you to be accosted by the fellow – though I clearly laid down the rules that my agents are free to come and go as they please – so I would recommend leaving by the back."

Only moments later, I had bundled myself up in my greatcoat and bowler and had descended the staircase and made my way out the back door. I made my way along the road until I came to the main thoroughfare and hailed a hansom. Once ensconced in the cab, I sat back and let the events of the day play out in my mind once more. It was cool in the cab; the autumn air had turned biting and cold quickly. The chill which passed over me only made my mission all the more tense. What was I to find, I asked myself. Though I was by no means won over by a supernatural theory, what horrors might await me at this house which was so shrouded in mystery and horror? These thoughts occupied me until my hansom drew up outside the very dwelling and

I alighted, feeling, for an instant, unsteady as my boot touched the cobblestone pavement.

The road was narrow, lined on both sides by buildings of a small, but comfortable-looking nature. A set of neat steps ascended towards the doors of each building and, should there not have been a constable posted outside the door to number 41, I should have figured that it was just as innocuous a residence as any other building on the boulevard. I slowly approached the uniformed officer, and I could see his face – a youthful countenance with a large nose and bushy mustache – register a look of familiarity with my own person. All the same, it was evident that the man could not place my name.

"Sorry, sir," he said, "no one's allowed in."

"But I have come under the express orders of –"

Before I could finish, the door to number 41 Hamilton Gardens opened behind the constable and the youthful Inspector Stanley Hopkins faced me in the doorway. "Dr. Watson! I must confess that I am not very surprised to find you here!"

"Good evening, inspector," I replied. "I take it then that you have been reading the latest edition of *The Star*."

Hopkins patted in his inner breast pocket. "I just got through reading it. You know how I respect Mr. Holmes, but I must admit that I rather think his ego has gone to his head this time around. Step aside, Constable McWilliams. This man may come through."

Stanley Hopkins opened the door wider, and I stepped through the threshold and into the house. I found myself standing in a small foyer which opened up into a modest sitting room. It was furnished with a few chairs and a settee. A low fire burned in the grate on the opposite side of the room and, as I followed the inspector into the house, I saw the figure of a woman, dressed entirely in black, perched on the edge of the settee. She appeared to be gazing deeply into the undulating flames.

Hopkins cleared his throat and the woman turned about quickly. She was a tall, handsome woman; her beauty was not diminished by the redness around her eyes and the tears which still festooned them. Clothed entirely in black, I would have perceived the woman to be in mourning. Knowing her situation, however, I figured that she was not far afield from grieving.

"Mrs. Cardew," Hopkins said gently, "I would like to introduce you to Dr. John Watson. He is a personal friend of mine, as well as the friend and biographer of Mr. Sherlock Holmes, the detective."

"How do you do, madam?" I asked. I took her hand in mine. Her grip was weak and, considering her dainty appendage, the lady seemed suddenly very fragile to me.

"It is a pleasure to meet you," she replied softly. "I had read that Mr. Holmes has taken an interest in Lillian's case."

"He most certainly has," I replied. "I am here acting on Holmes's behalf."

"I am desperate to get this matter settled, Dr. Watson," Mrs. Cardew replied. She returned to her seat on the settee and gestured for me to take a seat in one of the chairs. I did so as she withdrew a handkerchief from the folds of her black dress and dabbed at her eyes. "Can I be of assistance to you or Mr. Holmes in anyway?"

I was not sure how to advance from here. Holmes's instructions were vague in the extreme. I found myself now with little idea how to proceed. The overwhelming sense of dread which had seemed to settle over the household did nothing to ease my nerves. I suddenly remembered how keen Holmes had been to see photographs of the mother and daughter and the mission which he had given me.

"Perhaps you can be of assistance to us, Mrs. Cardew," I replied. "Do you have any photographs of you with your daughter?"

"Oh, of course," she said. She rose from the settee and moved further into the sitting room. I stood and joined her at a small bureau. It was covered with an assortment of papers and, atop it, two framed pictures of the mother and daughter. I could see new tears welling up in Mrs. Cardew's eyes.

"These photographs are my only solace now," she said as she pressed her handkerchief to her eye again. "Only this afternoon that reporter, Mr. Parker, came around and asked if he might borrow one of these photos. I refused and told him that these photographs were the only memories of the little girl I so love."

I knew that Holmes would be pleased to hear that Parker had made the attempt. However, seeing as I was playing the part of the understanding supporter, I was obligated to exclaim: "The nerve of the fellow!"

Mrs. Cardew returned the frame to the bureau top and turned on me suddenly. "Oh, Dr. Watson! Will my little girl ever be better? I don't care what has caused her to act this way. I simply want her to be the same, smiling child whom I raised for eleven years."

"I am confident that she will recover," I replied. I gently took hold of her hand once more and patted it. "Some of England's finest minds have taken an interest in this case. I am certain that your little girl will be returned to you."

I nimbly reached out my other arm and, with an amount of stealth which I think would have impressed even the most seasoned of thieves; I slipped the picture into the folds of my coat.

"Thank you, Dr. Watson," she said. "Is there anything else which I may do to assist you?"

"I think not," I replied.

I turned to Stanley Hopkins. "There have been no developments, I take it?"

"I'm afraid not, doctor. Dr. Flaughtery called 'round earlier this evening to tend to Lillian. He's still upstairs now. He has come up with nothing, I'm afraid."

Though I knew that it was hardly my place to interfere, I took pity on the poor woman. I knew as a doctor I had to help her in some capacity and, perhaps without knowing entirely what I was saying, I had asked if I could take a look at Lillian Cardew. The faintest ghost of a smile crossed across the edges of Mrs. Cardew's mouth.

"You said yourself that some of England's finest minds have taken an interest in my daughter's case," she said. "As a despondent mother, I would not be doing all that is in my power to see her get better if I denied one more of England's finest minds to examine my girl."

I politely waved away Mrs. Cardew's compliment. I cast a nod to Hopkins who slightly nodded his head in approval. Then, gesturing for Mrs. Cardew to lead the way, I followed her to the narrow staircase. As I mounted the steps behind her, I suddenly felt an overwhelming sense of dread overtake me. With each step I felt myself nearing the spot of the strange goings-on which had captivated and horrified this country. What was I to find on the other side of the door leading to Lillian Cardew's room? As we reached the top step, I felt a numbness surround my legs. I took hold of the wooden banister to support myself.

Mrs. Cardew tapped on the door. From within, I heard a man's voice call out and we stepped inside. The man I took to be Dr. Flaughtery when I saw him standing over the girl's bed. He held a dainty wrist between his fingers and stood looking at the hands of a watch tick away before him. He put the watch back into his waistcoat pocket, and gently returned Lillian Cardew's arm to her side on the bed. She was wrapped in her sheets which covered all of her petite frame in a tight shroud.

"Doctor," Mrs. Cardew said addressing Flaughtery, "I would like to introduce you to Dr. John Watson. He asked if he could examine Lillian."

"By all means, Doctor," Flaughtery replied, stepping away from the bed.

I approached the bedsides and, what happened next still haunts me to this day. In a swift movement which caught everyone in the room off-guard, Lillian Cardew jumped up from her lying position and stood upon the bed. It was Lillian Cardew, but one could be forgiven for thinking otherwise as she looked nothing like the pleasant, little girl who had stood dutifully by her mother's side in the photograph I had seen only moments ago. She was wrapped in her nightdress and her hair stuck out wildly in all directions. Beneath her dark locks which covered her face, I could still see her eyes which had gone over white. She gnashed her teeth together like some wild animal and, before I could move, she had jumped from her bed and leapt at me.

I confess that fear had rooted me to the spot and the girl grabbed hold of my arm as she had launched herself into the air. Pandemonium broke out as both Flaughtery and Mrs. Cardew rushed to my side; both were affecting to pry the little girl from my sleeve. Lillian Cardew let out a guttural snarl, not unlike the hiss of an angry crocodile – a sound which I am unlikely to forget from my days passing through India.

The two managed to wrench Lillian Cardew from my arm, but once they had done so, she spun around and lashed out at the doctor. I saw her fingers connect with his cheek and he tumbled backwards; the traces of the scratch marks crimson on his face. He fell backwards as Stanley Hopkins rushed up the stairs and stood in the threshold of the room, his gaze locked on the strange tableau within. Composing himself quite quickly, Hopkins rushed into the room and took hold of Lillian. Together, we endeavored to force the girl back onto the bed and, as we held her down, Flaughtery regained his composure, stood, rummaged through his Gladstone bag, produced a syringe and, rushing forward to Lillian, he thrust the needle into her arm and pushed the piston down. She went limp only seconds later, leaving the three of us to stand around in shock and exhaustion.

"The sedative I gave her should keep her out for a few hours," Flaughtery said breathlessly.

"What came over her?" Mrs. Cardew asked.

"I have no idea," Dr. Flaughtery responded. He dabbed at his bleeding cheek with his own handkerchief and endeavored to catch his breath. "She was like a wild animal. I've never seen a person do anything like it this side of an asylum door."

The doctor's words did nothing for Mrs. Cardew. She made her way out of the room and silently descended the staircase back to the sitting room. Hopkins and I followed shortly behind and, when we found our way into the sitting room, Mrs. Cardew had sunk once more onto the settee and was convulsing with an onslaught of fresh tears.

The whole scene left me in a state of utter stupefaction and I took my leave. There was nothing that I was looking forward to more than a drink and the warm fire of Baker Street.

As I rode homeward, ensconced once more in a hansom cab, I knew that my dreams would be haunted by the face of Lillian Cardew. I was inclined to agree with Dr. Flaughtery as I sat back against the plush interior of the hansom. I had never seen any person act the way the little girl did that night. Though I was loath to admit it, I – only for an instant – entertained the notion that some supernatural hand may have played a role in this bad business. Was this evidence, I wondered as the cab drew up outside of 221b Baker Street, that the devil can play a hand in the affairs of men?

"It certainly sounds as if you had an eventful evening," Sherlock Holmes said, more cheerily than I would have liked, at the conclusion of my tale. He was wrapped in his preferred dressing gown and stretched out before the fire, filling his pipe with tobacco from the Persian slipper while I sat opposite and nursed a brandy.

Lighting a match and applying it to the bowl of his pipe, Holmes tossed the stub into the fire and sat, pulling on his pipe for what seemed like an eternity. "You will," he said at length, "be glad to hear that my evening here proved to be quite fruitful as well."

"Oh? Why was that?"

"The photograph," Holmes replied. "It was, as I thought, quite illuminating."

Standing, Holmes moved to the breakfast table where he picked up the picture which I absconded with and pressed it into my hand. I stared into the content faces of Mrs. Cardew and Lillian. Nothing about them seemed to suggest the misery and hardship which both now endured. Had Sherlock Holmes been in one of his more philosophical moods, I might have made a comment about the hand of fate, but I resisted. I handed the photograph back to my friend.

"The picture was of use then?"

"It was invaluable," Holmes said with a grin. "It truly was the missing piece."

"You've solved it then?"

Holmes held his index finger aloft. "Not yet," he said. "This development has raised a question or two of its own which I endeavored to answer this evening. I have sent a few telegrams and – with luck – I shall receive an answer to all of them on the morrow."

I downed the last of my brandy. "Well, go on Holmes, let me hear it through!"

"Ah, I am afraid that you shall have to wait, my dear Watson. As I mentioned the case hinges upon a number of pieces of conjecture and it would be remiss of me should I tell you my solution without facts to support it. Besides, you ought to know me well enough that I cannot resist a touch of the dramatic. The denouement of this affair will take place here, in this very room, tomorrow evening."

Holmes returned his attention to the photo. He seemed to consider it intently for some time before I heard him murmur, nearly inaudibly under his breath: "She does look quite young, doesn't she?"

I stared up at Holmes from my seat, my attention arrested by his cryptic comment. "Lillian Cardew?" I asked.

"Yes," Holmes replied. "She *is* quite young."

"The girl is only eleven years old," I countered, not a little peeved at my friend's usual, enigmatic manner.

"Is she?" came his unexpected reply.

So saying, Holmes laid his pipe aside and moved away from his chair. "It has been a rather taxing day or the both of us," he said. "I would suggest a good night's rest. I shall see you in the morning, Watson."

Crossing to his room, Holmes stepped inside and closed the door behind him. I huffed. Sometimes, I told myself, Sherlock Holmes could be the most infuriating of men. Despite what we had both been through that day, he still refused to share his results. However, I knew Holmes's methods well enough by now not to be too upset. I poured myself another glass of brandy and stared into the flames in the fireplace for some time. Nodding off, I roused myself and made my way to my bed.

It was a fitful sleep which came to me that evening. Visions of Lillian Cardew still burned in my memory like an ember. I recall that I woke more than once during the seemingly endless night. I could still hear the hisses which the little girl made. I could see her eyes which had gone over white. Finally, knowing that sleep would never truly come, I rose early, washed, dressed, and made my way to our sitting room. I sat about with a book for some time before Mrs. Hudson brought a pot of hot coffee which did go some way to restoring my spirits after the sleepless evening.

Per his habit, Holmes slept late and, when he did sweep into the sitting room, he seemed cheery and in good sorts. We breakfasted and, at the conclusion of our meal, he moved to his usual chair and spread the first edition of the paper across his knee.

"This is a most curious development," he said.

Passing the page to me, I read the bold headline:

Famed Haunted House Burns in Mysterious Fire

"Good lord," I murmured.

"Would you be so kind as to read the article, Watson?" It ran:

Number 41 Hamilton Gardens of St. John's Wood which has, of late, gained some reputation as a haunted house following a series of disturbances, garnering much public attention, caught fire in the early hours of the morning. The only occupants of the house, Mrs. Emily Cardew and her eleven-year-old daughter, Lillian, are, as yet, unaccounted for. Inspector Stanley Hopkins of Scotland Yard – who was already posted at the house following the series of disturbances –

refused to comment whether the family is believed to have perished in the flames.

The matter of the supposed haunting of number 41 Hamilton Gardens has incited some public interest in the past few weeks. Noted spiritualist Sir Jeffery Curbishly has been involved in the matter as has the famed detective, Mr. Sherlock Holmes.

"I would not be surprised in the slightest if Sir Jeffrey uses this development to his advantage," Holmes said once I had finished reading. "To Sir Jeffrey, there are no earthly occurrences. That fire was not an accident, nor was it caused by some human hand. Surely, it was the devil who burned the house down, bathing his demonic disciples in hellfire!"

"Do you think they perished in the fire, Holmes?"

"Unlikely in the extreme," Holmes retorted. "And now, I must wait until I receive the answers to my telegrams. I am, unfortunately, working against the unstoppable forces of bureaucratic red tape. An answer could be hours away."

Holmes wordlessly moved to his chemical apparatus and continued to work in quiet.

Busying himself with his test tubes and beakers, he sat in silence as I finished perusing the paper. Only a quarter of an hour had elapsed before there came a ring from the door below. Holmes sat up, a grin crossing his usually cruel mouth. Standing, he opened the door and met Mrs. Hudson at the threshold, relieving her of our visitor's card which she carried upon a small, silver tray. Holmes studied the card and, wordlessly gestured for our landlady to show the guest in.

Holmes turned to me and smiled like a cat that had just eaten a canary. "An answer to one of my telegrams has come sooner than anticipated, Watson."

A moment later, Holmes greeted a tall, distinguished-looking woman at the top of the stairs and showed her into the sitting room where he briefly introduced me and then took his place before the fire.

"You might be interested to know, Watson, that our distinguished guest is Mrs. Henrietta Cardew, mother of the late Lieutenant Cardew. I contacted her last evening and she has done me a tremendous service by replying as promptly as she did."

Though I perceived that the woman who drew into our sitting room would have normally held herself with a regal bearing, she moved into the room slowly and under great duress. She had stripped off her white gloves and held them tightly in her hands, wringing them anxiously. I knew at once that the poor woman was consumed with thoughts for her daughter-in-law and beloved grandchild.

"I extend my thoughts and best wishes to you, Mrs. Cardew," I said, as Holmes gently led the woman to the settee. "I know how trying this morning's news must be for you."

"It is only because I know that you are so intimately associated with all of this terrible business, Mr. Holmes, that I came as quickly as I did. Therefore, if I can be of any service to you, Mr. Holmes, it would take a great weight off of my mind. Emily had been so consumed by the tragic events which have surrounded her and Lillian for the past few weeks. I truly fear for her. She had shut herself away completely and refused to see me."

"Her actions surprised you no doubt?"

"They most certainly did," Mrs. Henrietta Cardew replied. "But, I suppose, I can understand her."

"I understand it that you have been providing Emily Cardew with something of an allowance ever since the untimely death of your son."

"I have, Mr. Holmes," Henrietta Cardew said, seeming to take umbrage with Holmes's questioning tone. "Emily was quite beside herself after my son's death. What's more, there was a baby on the way. I felt morally objected to assist her in any way I could."

"And you have continued to look out for Lillian's interests to this day?"

"Why, of course I have. The dear, sweet girl deserves only the best in my mind."

Holmes drew himself up before the fire. "And how long did you intend to carry on financially supporting Emily and Lillian?"

"Mr. Holmes," the woman said impetuously, "I fail to see the point –"

Holmes quieted the woman with a look.

"I had intended to support Lillian until she was of legal age, of course."

Sherlock Holmes crossed to the table and plucked the framed picture from the tabletop. "Mrs. Cardew, the question I am about to pose to you will seem unusual, but would you be so kind as to identify the woman in this photograph?"

Holmes handed the photograph to the woman and she stared at it intently. "It's Emily," she said. "But who is -?"

"Who is the young girl with her?" Holmes asked.

"Yes," she replied, her tone wavering, filled with confusion.

Holmes took the photo from Mrs. Cardew's hand and returned it to the table. "Thank you very much, Mrs. Cardew. You have indeed been of invaluable assistance to my case."

With a few words of reassurance, Holmes managed to cajole the woman to follow him out of the room and, once he had bundled her away in a cab, he returned to the sitting room where I still sat, my face a mask of bewilderment.

"What is the meaning of all this, Holmes?"

"All in good time," Holmes retorted.

It was only moments after our last guest had departed that the bell chimed below once again. Holmes saved Mrs. Hudson the trouble of having to mount the seventeen steps to our sitting room by greeting the guest in the foyer. I moved to the door and heard my friend exclaim pleasantly as he opened the door and guided our client through. I was greeted by the sight of Holmes guiding an austere-looking woman into our sitting room where he gestured for her to sit.

"Miss Primm," he said, "you have, as I understand it, been in charge of the St. Isidore Home for Children for the past twenty years."

The woman peered over the top of the delicate pince-nez which she wore on her pallid face. "You understand quite well, Mr. Holmes."

"Excellent," Holmes replied. "I realize the question which I posed to you in my telegram is one you may be hesitant to answer, but it is imperative to solve a baffling mystery and it will bring to book two dangerous scoundrels: did a woman going by the name of either Cardew or Melville adopt a child from your foundling home eleven years ago?"

Miss Primm shifted uncomfortably in her chair. She drew in a very deep breath as she stared, fixated at one point upon the carpet before she said, "You should consider yourself quite lucky, Mr. Holmes, that when I received your telegram early this morning I consulted my register at once. I can tell you most definitely that a woman answering to the name of Melville adopted a girl from our home."

"This girl," Holmes pressed, "what was she like?"

"Oh, she was a lovely baby," Miss Primm said, her grim countenance lightening as she reminisced. "She was a beautiful girl, though rather sickly, I'm afraid. But, Miss Melville seemed like such a caring young woman that we had no qualms whatsoever in sending the girl off with her."

"Thank you," Holmes said. His face was a mask as he showed Miss Primm to the door. Then, silently he returned to his chemical apparatus.

Knowing that this would occupy him for the remainder of the morning, I decided that there was nothing for me to do but decamp to my club. I set out and, as I hailed a hansom, I cast a glance across the street. I could still see Curbishly's man standing on the opposite side of the road, his eye still fixed upon the window of our sitting room. I chuckled in spite of myself as I rode off.

I spent my morning and afternoon in solitude. I perused the papers at length and sampled a fine port. I also played billiards with my customary partner, Thurston. His attempts to spark conversation regarding the Hamilton Gardens business were not as fruitful as he would have wished; I am sure, for I was unable to supply him with any true answers.

It was nearing five and I was making my way out of the club when I happened to catch sight of the latest edition of *The Star*. Its front page leading article declared – just as Holmes had surmised – that Sir Jeffrey Curbishly had put forth a supernatural explanation for the house fire. Hailing another hansom, I rode back to Baker Street, keenly aware that my long wait to hear Holmes's explanation of the case was almost at an end.

I never did suspect our sitting room to be as full as it was when I arrived. Holmes stood before the fireplace while Stanley Hopkins had taken my friend's customary chair. Mr. Parker was seated in my own seat and Sir Jeffrey Curbishly sat uncomfortably on the sofa.

"Glad that you have joined us, Watson," Holmes said airily. "I am just about to present my explanation for the Hamilton Gardens business."

I took a seat at the breakfast table and, once Parker had extracted his notebook from his inner pocket, Holmes drew himself up and began.

"From the beginning," said Holmes, "I never believed that there was anything remotely supernatural about the Hamilton Gardens business. Though the case did appear to have some fanciful aspects, I resolutely believed that this was the work of some person. The only person – or persons – who could have been responsible was Mrs. Cardew and her daughter. I did not know how or why they would do this. That is, until I happened to make a chance remark about 'the prosperous con artist trade.' This, in itself, was what truly started the cogs working in my mind. Mrs. Emily Cardew and her daughter were not what they appeared.

"But, I asked myself, why should they wish to create an elaborate ruse about demonic possession? As Mr. Parker told me, Mrs. Cardew was quite well-off financially. Her late father had a position in Her Majesty's Government and she was supported by the family of her late husband. Their house was situated in one of the upper class regions of the city, meaning that the family was not trying to move from their quarters. Despite all of this, I knew something for certain:

the appeal of money can persist even when one is well off. Simply put, gentlemen, we have been witness to one of the most elaborate and deceptive schemes which I have ever witnessed.

"Once I began to question the character of Mrs. Cardew and her daughter, I sent a telegram to my brother, Mycroft. He occupies a position in Her Majesty's government and I wondered if any such person as Mr. Melville, Mrs. Cardew's father, existed. He responded to me only hours ago and told me that there was no record of anyone by the name of Melville having occupied any governmental position. This lie was only the first in a series. I sent another telegram to the public records office and requested a birth certificate for Lillian Cardew. They too had no record.

"Prior to her marriage to Lieutenant Cardew, what do we know about Emily? It appears as though those specifics were fraudulent in the extreme. Mrs. Cardew is no longer the long-suffering woman Mr. Parker portrayed her as, but instead a woman whose past is a mystery. Having borne no child, one wonders just who Lillian Cardew is. It was for that simple reason that I wanted to see a photograph of the young woman and her daughter. Perhaps you gentlemen are unaware, but one of the simplest methods to determine someone's age is to simply look at his or her face. Between the ages of twenty-five and thirty-five, the first few visible lines of age are evident around the eyes and on the forehead. While I knew that it would be a challenge to determine this from a photograph alone, I figured that it would be the best method of age identification for me without leaving this room."

Holmes crossed to the breakfast table and once more picked up the photograph. He plucked his convex lens from his inner pocket and held the glass directly over the picture. "Though it is difficult to perceive," he said, "the faintest lines around the eyes and forehead are visible to my lens on the face of Lillian Cardew. Lillian Cardew was not Emily's child, gentlemen. Rather, her sister."

There was an audible intake of breath from everyone in the room.

"The ruse was one of the simplest variety. Did I not comment last evening, Watson that Lillian Cardew truly did look like a little girl of eleven? No one would have questioned her for an instant.

"After I had determined that Lillian Cardew was also not who she appeared to be, I spent my evening poring over some of my indexes and clippings. I came across a reference to a pair of sisters – performers – who were quite popular in small, traveling venues throughout England. The younger sister was particularly popular. She appeared to be a young girl despite being in her early twenties. She was also an accomplished contortionist. You will doubtlessly recall the words of Mrs. Ellen Mortimer: 'little Lillian Cardew convulsed wildly on her bed. It was as though she was a puppet being conducted by some great, invisible hand pulling at strings from above.' An eleven-year-old girl could not have acted in such a way, but a limber twenty-year-old certainly could.

"As I followed this line of investigation, I found that these sisters had left the sideshow and had married. It was something of a disappointment to ardent appreciators of vaudeville, though the sisters returned to the stage only a year later. What had become of the marriage no one knows, however their spouses were surely only the first in their schemes: find a financially stable young man, marry him, collect his money, and leave him shortly thereafter. However, this time around they played too bold a game.

"This morning I questioned Lieutenant Cardew's mother, Mrs. Henrietta Cardew. She told me that she planned on continuing to support both Emily and Lillian until Lillian grew to legal age. Therefore, Emily has the perfect avenue by which to elicit money from her late husband's family for many years. I believe that Emily grew to be financially dependent upon the Cardews and, would have continued to live in a manner to which she had become quite accustomed had the real Lillian Cardew not died."

"What on earth do you mean, Mr. Holmes?" Parker cried.

"Consider gentlemen: there must have been a real Lillian Cardew. Mr. Parker told me that Emily was close to the Cardew family, a fact which was substantiated by Mrs. Cardew herself. What's more, I also spoke to the head of the Saint Isidore Foundling Home this morning who informed me that about eleven years ago, a young woman calling herself Melville adopted a young girl. This could, one supposes, be coincidence, but I do not give credence to such theories. The links in the chain of events were beginning to be forged.

"What Emily did not anticipate, however, was that her child was a sickly one. Doubtlessly, the girl succumbed to some illness, but Emily was not prepared to lose the cash-flow which her mother-in-law continued to pay to her and her daughter. Emily persisted the falsehood that her daughter was alive and well, moving into Hamilton Gardens and having her sister impersonate her daughter. To further the distance between her and the Cardew family, they concocted the elaborate scheme of demonic possession. It was all rather more *Grand Guignol* than they anticipated, I believe, but it did suffice. That is until the popular press became involved."

"But how could we have fallen for their story?" Parker asked.

"That was the simplest part of it all," Holmes replied. "Though I applaud your work as a journalist, Mr. Parker, I am afraid that even you did not question all aspects of your story. You did – as all journalists do – followed the tantalizing story to its source and never quite looked back. I would also not be surprised if you were taken in by Mrs. Cardew. You told me that you found her to be quite a handsome woman. I know that I am the exception to the rule, as most men do not allow their brains to govern their hearts. What's more, I shouldn't be surprised if Mrs. Mortimer, the witness to Lillian Cardew's *possessed* antics, were not chosen at random. You told me that Mrs. Mortimer called herself a 'God-fearing' woman who regularly attended church. It was not an out-of-character act to suggest that a priest be brought in to perform an exorcism.

"And lastly, there was Sir Jeffrey Curbishly. Sir Jeffrey's theories regarding demons from beyond our world excited the public and gave you much fodder to report on, Parker. In cases like this, the power of the press can be quite a force."

"But about the fire?" Stanley Hopkins asked.

"The fire was doubtlessly set deliberately," Holmes replied. "As I do not routinely number modesty among the virtues, I feel quite at liberty saying that as soon as Mr. Parker's article went to print saying that I would deliver a solution to the mystery in twenty-four hours' time, Emily and Lillian Cardew knew they had to act quickly. I would not be surprised, Inspector, should you make a formal examination of Mrs. Cardew's bank account, that you will find it empty. Obviously, they took off with their money and burned the house down only to further the claims that this business was not of an earthly origin."

"Incredible," I heard Parker murmur as he furiously took notes, "absolutely incredible!"

"I would imagine that Emily and Lillian Cardew will find England an inhospitable place," Holmes continued as he lit a cigarette. "They are, after all, quite well known. I would be very much surprised if they have not taken the boat train for the Continent."

Slipping his watch from his waistcoat pocket, Holmes continued, "They have quite a head start Inspector, but I am quite confident in your abilities should you wish to give chase."

"I think I shall do just that," Stanley Hopkins said as he jumped from his seat. He shook Holmes by the hand and a moment later he was out the door and bounding down the steps.

"And I think I had best be getting this story to my editor," said Parker.

Parker made his way out of the room. Sir Jeffrey Curbishly stood, his eyes filled with contempt, saying more than he could ever hope to verbalize. He made his exit in virtual silence. Once he had gone, Holmes closed the door behind him.

"Not a bad way to while away two days' time, eh, Watson?"

"That was quite clever of you, Holmes. Well done."

Sherlock Holmes slipped into his customary seat once more. "It really was a simple business once I managed to look beyond the sensational dressing. I believe this case was the perfect showcase to support one of my little sayings: As a rule, the more bizarre a thing is, the less mysterious it proves to be."

"I'm inclined to think that you're quite right," I replied.

Holmes tossed his cigarette into the fire. He stared into the flame for what seemed like an age. "The pair were quite the devious duo. But, on to other matters. You will have no doubt observed me hard at work for the past two days at my chemicals. I have recently become engaged in another case which is proving to be far more difficult. Allow me ten minutes to give you the pertinent details, my friend, and then, provided that Sir Jeffrey was kind enough to call off his watchdog across the way, I would find your assistance at the scene most invaluable."

Acknowledgements

This book has been a work in progress for many years. Perhaps longer than I ever realized. Since I first discovered Sherlock Holmes and Dr. Watson in the pages of *The Great Illustrated Classic* edition of *The Adventures of Sherlock Holmes*, I have wanted to uncover more mysteries for the Great Detective to solve. I suppose I was writing pastiches even before I could properly spell 'Moriarty' or 'hansom cab' and certainly before I ever knew what the word 'pastiche' meant. I like to think that I came a long way since then, and I have done so with the help of a number of people.

I am indebted to both my parents who nurtured my love for Holmes ever since the age of six. They bought me a deerstalker hat for my ninth birthday (to save me from stealing baseball caps from around the house to make my own) and more recently have done their best to make sure that I have enough bookshelf space to accommodate my ever-growing collection of Sherlockian books, films, and assorted odds-and-ends. Without their support, Holmes and Watson probably would not have remained the constant companions they are today.

When it came to the actual writing of these stories, I must thank David Marcum to who gave me my first real opportunity to write pastiches. He accepted "The Adventure of the Traveling Corpse" for the sixth volume of his excellent, ongoing anthology series *The MX Book of New Sherlock Holmes Stories* and three of the stories in this collection appeared in those books first. David was also kind enough to pass an eye over the initial manuscript for this book and give it his seal of approval.

My thanks also go out to Catharine Carmody for reading initial drafts of many of these stories. Her comments helped immeasurably, and she also single-handedly taught me how to use commas.

Ruby Brown I must thank for giving me the idea of a painter who is caught red-handed for a portrait he has painted. Some ideas are so good that they stick with you for years.

I must also thank Dr. Stacey Aronow, Ms. Elise Brand, and Miss Blair Endy, high school teachers who were among the first to support my Sherlockian writing, and who hosted an event at the school to celebrate the publication of my first short story.

Thanks to a few important people who I will sadly never have the opportunity to meet: Messrs. Basil Rathbone, Peter Cushing, and Jeremy Brett who were superstars for me when most kids my age were idolizing flash-in-the-pan teen pop stars. These gentlemen embodied Sherlock Holmes for me when I was growing up, and I still think of them as the best of the best. They have all inspired my writing and their familiar countenances have all been in my head at one time or another as I sent Holmes rushing out into the night in search for clues.

Lastly, my thanks to Sir Arthur Conan Doyle. It goes without saying that without him this book – and the countless others which have brought me immense pleasure – would not exist. For at least fifteen years, Doyle's writing has fascinated me and still does to this day.

To me the game has been afoot ever since. And it always will be.

About the Author

Nick Cardillo has been a devotee of the Great Detective since the age of six. His first published short story, "The Adventure of the Traveling Corpse" was published in *The MX Book of New Sherlock Holmes Stories – Part VI: 2017 Annual* edited by David Marcum and further Sherlockian adventures have appeared in subsequent volumes. Nick is a fan of The Golden Age of Detective Fiction, Hammer Horror, and *Doctor Who* on top of being a film buff. You can read his reviews and analyses of movies new and old on his blog, Sacred Celluloid. He is a student at Susquehanna University in Selinsgrove, Pennsylvania.

Also from MX Publishing

MX Publishing is the world's largest specialist Sherlock Holmes publisher, with over a hundred titles and fifty authors creating the latest in Sherlock Holmes fiction and non-fiction.

From traditional short stories and novels to travel guides and quiz books, MX Publishing cater for all Holmes fans.

The collection includes leading titles such as _Benedict Cumberbatch In Transition_ and _The Norwood Author_ which won the 2011 Howlett Award (Sherlock Holmes Book of the Year).

MX Publishing also has one of the largest communities of Holmes fans on Facebook with regular contributions from dozens of authors.

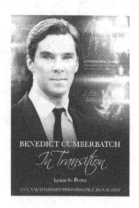

www.sherlockholmesbooks.com

Also from MX Publishing

 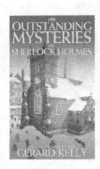 

Our bestselling books are our short story collections;

'Lost Stories of Sherlock Holmes' , 'The Outstanding
Mysteries of Sherlock Holmes', The Papers of Sherlock
Holmes Volume 1 and 2, 'Untold Adventures of Sherlock
Holmes' (and the sequel 'Studies in Legacy) and 'Sherlock
Holmes in Pursuit', 'The Cotswold Werewolf and Other
Stories of Sherlock Holmes' – and many more......

www.sherlockholmesbooks.com

263

Also from MX Publishing

"Phil Growick's, 'The Secret Journal of Dr Watson', is an adventure which takes place in the latter part of Holmes and Watson's lives. They are entrusted by HM Government (although not officially) and the King no less to undertake a rescue mission to save the Romanovs, Russia's Royal family from a grisly end at the hand of the Bolsheviks. There is a wealth of detail in the story but not so much as would detract us from the enjoyment of the story. Espionage, counter-espionage, the ace of spies himself, double-agents, double-crossers...all these flit across the pages in a realistic and exciting way. All the characters are extremely well-drawn and Mr Growick, most importantly, does not falter with a very good ear for Holmesian dialogue indeed. Highly recommended. A five-star effort."
The Baker Street Society

Also from MX Publishing

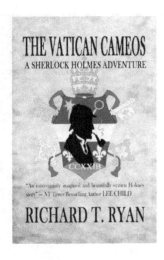

When the papal apartments are burgled in 1901, Sherlock Holmes is summoned to Rome by Pope Leo XII. After learning from the pontiff that several priceless cameos that could prove compromising to the church, and perhaps determine the future of the newly unified Italy, have been stolen, Holmes is asked to recover them. In a parallel story, Michelangelo, the toast of Rome in 1501 after the unveiling of his Pieta, is commissioned by Pope Alexander VI, the last of the Borgia pontiffs, with creating the cameos that will bedevil Holmes and the papacy four centuries later. For fans of Conan Doyle's immortal detective, the game is always afoot. However, the great detective has never encountered an adversary quite like the one with whom he crosses swords in "The Vatican Cameos.."

"An extravagantly imagined and beautifully written Holmes story"
(**Lee Child**, NY Times Bestselling author, Jack Reacher series)

Also from MX Publishing

The Conan Doyle Notes (The Hunt For Jack The Ripper)
"Holmesians have long speculated on the fact that the Ripper murders aren't mentioned in the canon, though the obvious reason is undoubtedly the correct one: even if Conan Doyle had suspected the killer's identity he'd never have considered mentioning it in the context of a fictional entertainment. Ms Madsen's novel equates his silence with that of the dog in the night-time, assuming that Conan Doyle did know who the Ripper was but chose not to say – which, of course, implies that good old stand-by, the government cover-up. It seems unlikely to me that the Ripper was anyone famous or distinguished, but fiction is not fact, and "The Conan Doyle Notes" is a gripping tale, with an intelligent, courageous and very likable protagonist in DD McGil."
The Sherlock Holmes Society of London

www.sherlockholmesbooks.com

CPSIA information can be obtained
at www.ICGtesting.com
Printed in the USA
BVHW071925011219
565292BV00001B/71/P